MW00329635

# ADVANCE PRAISE

"Walsh (*I Am Defiance*) again brings a powerful woman from history to life with this middle-grade adventure featuring 16-year-old Revolutionary War hero Sybil Ludington... Walsh's easy, flowing prose breathes life into colonial America. Readers will find themselves in the thick of the Revolutionary War as well as eighteenth-century living... Middle-grade historical fiction fans will be swept up in the bravery of one young woman's fight to save her country against a British attack."

— **Publishers Weekly**, BookLife *Editor's Pick*

"*By the Light of Fireflies* adds a unique female perspective to a time in our country's history that has been dominated by male voices. Jenni L. Walsh spins an engaging tale, artfully mixing historical fact with fiction that keeps the reader riveted from the first word to the last."

— **Misty Miller**, 5th Grade Teacher
Texas Virtual Academy Hallsville

"A historical gem, readers will enjoy learning about Revolutionary War heroine Sybil Ludington and her Patriotic ride. Just like Sybil Ludington sometimes we face a difficult journey which unlocks the courage, determination, and power that lives inside all of us. I can't wait to share this book with my fifth grade readers and writers."

— **Ginette Garrity**, 5th Grade ELA Teacher,
Byram Intermediate School

"Middle grade fiction readers will find *By the Light of the Fireflies* a fine historical novel based on the life of a Colonial girl... As Sybil steps into a role she'd never envisioned, young readers receive an action-packed story that captures the environment and atmosphere of the times... Jenni L. Walsh is especially adept at capturing Sybil's first-person observations and emotions...These drive a story line that personalizes the history in a manner that makes it understandable, realistic, and quite accessible... Middle grade readers who normally eschew fact-laden historical fiction will find the emotional driving force particularly strong in *By the Light of the Fireflies*. This approach strengthens the compelling story of a young girl's trials, which forces her into the unexpected role of becoming a female war hero in times where girls and women normally are staid." — **Midwest Book Review**

"Perfect for 3rd-5th grade readers, especially those who shy away from lengthier books. Jenni L. Walsh tells the story masterfully!" — **Galiah Morgenstern**, Educator

"Wow, what a suspenseful, adventure this book was! Sybil's dad talks about the magic of fireflies, and Sybil finds fireflies helping her out when she least expected to see them, in her need to help her family during the Revolutionary War. Sybil becomes a heroine in many ways, and George Washington even thanks her for her heroism as a messenger for the Continental Army. This will make a great read aloud. Such a great book!" — **Vicky VanFradenburgh**, Educator

"Brilliant retelling of Sybil's story. I promise that you will stand up and cheer Sybil on throughout her nighttime adventure and gasp at the twists and turns in this story." — **Christie Omasta**, Educator

# BY THE LIGHT OF FIREFLIES

# BY THE LIGHT OF FIREFLIES

A Novel of War Hero
Sybil Ludington

## JENNI L. WALSH

*Wyatt-MacKenzie Publishing*
DEADWOOD, OREGON

By the Light of Fireflies
A Novel of War Hero Sybil Ludington
Jenni L. Walsh

Hardcover ISBN:9781954332126
Softcover ISBN: 9781954332133
Ebook ISBN: 9781954332164

Library of Congress Control Number: 2021943326

Wyatt-MacKenzie Publishing, Inc.
Deadwood, Oregon
www.WyattMacKenzie.com

*For Sybil—the little-known young heroine
of the Revolutionary War.*

# CHAPTER 1

They were coming for us.

The Loyalists.

Loyal to the King of England.

In the woods outside our home, their voices cackled, hooted, and hollered. They screamed, "Traitor!"

I trembled. They were talking about Papa. He was *not* loyal to King George III. Once upon a time, Papa had been. He had served in the King's army. But Papa didn't side with the British anymore. Not with how England was treating the new American colonies. Taxing us, not giving us a say on anything, forcing us to let their armed soldiers live and quarter in our homes.

"Traitor!" I heard again, from where I stood at the window at the bend of our staircase, weak at the knees, my hands clutching the windowsill for support.

Mama had feared they'd come. Papa had been offered a captain position from the British governor of New York. Papa had said no.

Outside, I couldn't see the men. Too many trees obscured them, hid them. But they were out there in the wintry night, their voices carrying through the oaks and pines. I pictured torches illuminating their angry faces. Had they come to hoot and holler to simply scare and taunt Papa? Or were they here to punish him? Would they break the tree line, enter our clearing, and approach our home ….

I shuddered away the remainder of my thought.

I shuddered away what their fire could do to our house.

Papa's voice rung out. "Into the cellar. All of you!"

The sounds of Mama and my five siblings echoed through the house.

A chill ran down my spine and I rubbed my arms. But my eyes stayed glued on the dark night. The reason was simple: I ached to see the lights of the fireflies.

Papa insisted they were magical. Enchanted.

Just last week, he'd said, "I was around your same age— maybe eleven or twelve—when *my* papa first told me about the magic of the fireflies."

"The *what*?" I'd asked.

Papa was a big, burly man. A trained soldier. And there he was talking about magic? At my squinted, questioning eyes, a mischievous smile had spread on Papa's face. "Didn't you know? Fireflies are magic, Sybil."

He had said it so matter-of-factly, but then a whimsical yet frightening story poured from his mouth. "I was only fifteen, in the middle of a battle … one where I thought all was lost. Picture me: on my belly. It was dark, the only light coming from the moon and sparks of gunfire."

I had shivered at the danger he'd been in.

"I didn't know which way I was crawling, but my superiors were calling for us to retreat. I thought I'd never get off the battlefield without a miracle. That was when I thought of the story my own Papa told me about the fireflies and how they come at different times, for different reasons. Sometimes, they simply talk to one another. Nothing special. But if you see them in ways you're not supposed to"—Papa had whistled—"that's *special*. That means they've come to talk to *you*. They flash to tell us something important, Sybil."

"And you saw them?"

"Oh I saw them all right. It was the dead of winter and I saw them. They're supposed to be underground at that time of the year, not yet fireflies, but still tiny glow worms. Yet there they were, blinking, silently talking to *me*, telling me I was going to be all right, while gunfire exploded all around me. Still I was frozen in place. That was when they showed me even more of their magic: They flickered in unison. It was unbelievable to see them doing that." He'd shaken his head. "It was like they were telling me to follow them. I listened and I found a hollow. There, I waited out the battle. And, I survived."

My mouth had hung open.

Now, I bit my lip, staring out the window. I'd seen fireflies flickering and chattering to each other before. But only in the summertime, when they were *supposed* to be there.

Tonight, though ….

Tonight—in a winter month, just like it'd been in Papa's story—I wanted to believe in the magic of the fireflies. I wished more than anything for the fireflies to appear. It'd mean something. It'd mean something *big*. It'd mean those Loyalists would come no closer to our home.

"Move!" my sister demanded.

But I couldn't move.

I was too scared to peel my eyes away from the window. Papa's story—still so fresh from hearing it only days ago—danced again through my mind.

"Don't just stand there. You're blocking the stairs," Rebecca growled. My sister let out a huff and pushed past me, one of my little brothers tucked into her side. "Mama won't be happy."

Mama wouldn't. I was the oldest. I was supposed to be helping her get my sleepy siblings downstairs to safety, especially with Mama as pregnant as she was.

The sounds outside grew.

High-pitched whistles.

Deep-sounding shouts.

I swallowed roughly.

Where were the fireflies? Would they come to save us?

I gripped the windowsill harder. Another brother rustled past me, tugging on my nightgown as he went.

But I stayed. I stared so hard into the trees, searching for the fireflies, that everything began to blur.

I covered my ears against the mob looming closer outside.

Then, I couldn't believe my eyes. I saw them. Flashing. Intermittently.

Between the trees, there were the fireflies.

Even while I had wished for them, I began to doubt Papa's story. It was only words, passed down in our family from Papa and from his Papa and from his Papa. But I so badly wanted to believe they'd show themselves when I needed their magic the most.

Now there they were.

*We're here!* they seemed to blink, when they were supposed to still be underground as glow worms.

My heart raced at the next flicker. Then another. They were undeniable, as more and more appeared.

I dropped my hands from my ears and yelled, "I see them!" I took three baby steps away from the window to lean over the stair's bannister and screamed, "Papa!"

His footsteps pounded, even louder than the voices outside, until he came into view on the ground floor. Perspiration had gathered on his forehead and stained his shirt. "What? What is it, Sybil?"

I told him to get up here, to hurry, to come see.

He barreled up the stairs, a musket clenched in his hand.

But by the time Papa reached me and I had turned back to the window, the fireflies had vanished. Poof. Gone.

"Fireflies!" I cried quickly. "They were here. Only a moment ago. They were here!"

With ragged breaths, Papa stood beside me, studying the dark night. He held up a finger, telling me to remain silent. Together, we looked, we listened.

Papa finally said, "Looks like the mob is gone, too."

A slow smile spread across his face, with wrinkles around his eyes.

"The fireflies?" I asked Papa.

He nodded. "The fireflies."

That night, I had wanted them to show themselves to tell me we'd be safe from the Loyalists. And they did. Papa had experienced a magical moment with the fireflies when he'd been a boy. And now, I'd had one, too. Only, the fireflies hadn't yet showed me all they could. There was more magic yet to come.

# CHAPTER 2

Now that I'd seen the majestic fireflies for myself, I had questions for Papa. He was resting an elbow on his shovel, wiping his brow despite the morning's almost freezing temperature. Mucking the chicken pen was hard work.

"Papa," I said, and he startled at my voice, before yawning. "Out of the two million people on this continent, how come the fireflies chose to appear early and help us?"

"Two million, huh?"

"That's my guess anyway."

Papa laughed. "Well, it's not that the fireflies chose to help us, per se. It's more that we choose them. *You* chose to believe they'd flash to tell you something important, right?"

"Right," I said. "Is that why I never saw them like that before? Because I didn't know about their magic until your story?"

"Like my Papa told me and I'm now telling you, those who believe are the people most likely to experience the enchantment of fireflies. It's only natural we look for them when we're in a moment of need. But I will say, what happened last night was pretty scary. I don't want it to happen again."

Me either.

Papa went on, "In fact, your mama is insisting I accept that captain position." He sunk his shovel into the hay. I rubbed my lips side to side, remembering the angry voices from last night and how they yelled *traitor*. "I've decided to accept the job."

"What?" I said before I could stop myself. I never questioned Papa. "But you're a Patriot now."

"Family comes first. And if me being a captain stops a repeat of last night, then so be it."

There was a glimmer in Papa's eye.

I narrowed mine.

He chuckled. "Okay, maybe my heart or head won't be in the job. But I'll do it for show."

"Sybil!" I heard, coming from the house. It was Rebecca. "You'll be late."

For school.

I glanced down our long drive. There was no sign of Johnny Whitaker yet. It was his routine to arrive every morning with his horse and cart to take Rebecca, Mary, and me to the church's schoolhouse. It was *my* routine to twist my mouth at him every time.

It wasn't that Johnny Whitaker was a pill. We'd grown up together, living close by, and he was actually quite funny. Just the other day he tipped his hat to us like he was taking us to a fancy ball, and nearly fell off the cart.

What bothered me was the simple fact that he was taking us to school. *He* was bringing us there when *I* was one hundred percent capable of driving the three miles to the church's school-house all on my own. Johnny Whitaker and I were the same age. We were the same height. Plus, we owned a farm cart and two horses.

However, Papa insisted those horses already had jobs. Jasper, with his thick chest and short legs, was used to plow the fields. And Pepper, thinner and longer, was better suited for riding. The real problem with Pepper, however, was that he'd only let Papa ride him. The sight of anyone else holding a saddle sent his legs running and his lips flapping.

My solution was quick: Let's get a third horse that I could use.

My parents' response was swift: *There's no need. We have Johnny Whitaker.*

Alas, it was a battle I never won. And I knew why. Johnny Whitaker was a boy and I was a girl. And Papa wanted a boy with his girls whenever we left our homestead.

"For your protection," he always said when I sulked.

There wasn't time for sulking this morning. I hurried inside to change for school. I kissed Mama good-bye, then the tops of my three brothers' heads. I wondered if Mama would have a boy or girl next. My two sisters and Johnny Whitaker were waiting for me when I rushed outside and onto Johnny's cart.

He had a whole mouthful of things he was saying. But I wasn't paying attention to him. We were clattering down the drive, each bump taking us farther from my house. We turned onto the ox-cart road and I was officially off our property. I knew there was a big world out there, proven by the seemingly endless number of trees I now saw. I took as much air into my lungs as possible, holding it there, doing my best to ignore the fact that any time I left the farm was when someone took me.

Still, I was always happy to cross that threshold, as if the moment I left our drive I transformed into Sybil the Unknown and Unexplored, instead of Sybil the Farmer's Daughter.

The drive to school was too quick, per usual.

At school, Johnny Whitaker extended a hand to my sister Mary to help her down from the cart. Rebecca would be next. When he was done unloading us, he'd leave. He used to stay for classes, but not anymore. Now he only dropped us off and picked us up. In the middle, he apprenticed with a blacksmith.

I envied him that, too. When I was a day over ten—the age when boys often began their apprenticeships—I asked Mama what I could be when I grew up. I didn't have many women in my life. My mama. The women at church. I knew what my mama did every day, but I didn't know what the church women did after the sermon was over. Maybe they led exciting lives that I never saw.

Mama had seemed surprised by my question. "Well, you'll get married."

"But then what? What job will I do?"

"My dear, you're a farmer's daughter and one day you'll be a farmer's wife. It's who we are. We stay on the farm. We have plenty of work of our own."

Funny, we lived on two hundred and twenty-nine acres of rolling land and even so, I felt suffocated. Confined. I still didn't understand why I couldn't be something different than I was born into.

At school, Johnny Whitaker extended his hand to help me

down from the cart, but I bunched my own skirts, quite capable of jumping down on my own. I was quite capable of a lot of things. Or I assumed I could be, if I were given a chance to try the things Johnny Whitaker would be allowed to do.

I could be a teacher. I sure loved facts.

Or maybe I could work as a cooper, making barrels and casks.

Maybe a cobbler. Everybody needed shoes.

Candles, too. So there was the option of a candle maker.

Or perhaps an apothecary, making medicine for people.

The idea of an innkeeper was interesting as well. It'd take me off the farm and put me in town or in a city, where I'd meet endless numbers of new people from faraway places. I bet they'd be dripping of stories to tell.

I wouldn't want to be a milliner, though. They made clothes to sell. That was my sister Rebecca's skill. Not mine. Even so, Mama had me sitting at the handloom and spinning wheel nearly every day to fashion clothes for our family.

The real problem, however, was that Mama insisted none of these jobs would be appropriate for me. Still, I dreamed. And, I wouldn't give up. Mama would hear about it again.

On the way inside the schoolhouse, I scoured the tall grass along the building for any fireflies trying to hide and sleep until nighttime. But I reminded myself their magic was needed to see them this time of year and I didn't have a need for my little friends at the moment, beyond simply wanting to see them again.

Inside the church's schoolhouse, Mr. Carter sat at his desk. Only a few chairs were filled so far. I placed both hands on his desk. "Good morning, Mr. Carter. Do you know anything about fireflies?"

He met my eyes, amusement there. "My brothers and I always called them lightning bugs."

Was that so?

"But they aren't bugs," he said. "They actually aren't flies either, if you're calling them fireflies. Flies have four wings, not two like fireflies, lightning bugs … whatever you want to call them. They're actually beetles."

Beetles, huh? I thanked Mr. Carter, and took my seat, still reveling in my newfound knowledge that those enchanted little creatures were actually beetles.

My day went on. Johnny Whitaker carted us home. I cooked and served supper, a pregnant Mama in bed from a long day. Then I entertained my brothers and sisters with hide-and-seek outside to keep the inside quiet for Mama, who was bound to have her baby any day now.

The next day went much the same. The days after, too, with the exception that hide-and-seek was replaced with things like jump rope, scotch-hopper, and rolling the hoop. And, on the days there wasn't school, I was assisting Papa and the farm help with getting the ground ready for plantings, then as the weeks passed, helping Papa with the plantings, while also trying to keep my brothers from rolling in the mud.

Not that I was successful—with the mud part. So I ended

up hauling the tub into the center of the kitchen, boiling water, putting one brother or sister in after the next. As always, I was the last to splash, when the bathwater was murky and straws of hay floated on the water's surface. And, now that Mama had her baby—a new baby brother—there'd be another sibling to go into the water before me.

Before I knew it, it was the dawn of summer, the time when the fireflies would begin to emerge from the ground. I couldn't sleep. I was too excited to see them again. That night, I crept outside. And, there they were blinking their hellos. It was like they knew I was coming to see them.

I went to bed with a smile.

I woke with a smile.

"Something's got you happy," Mama said to me. We stood together in front of the strawberry bushes. They were over-flowing with fruit.

I wouldn't dare tell Mama about my fascination with the fireflies. She'd only shake her head and tell me not to listen to Papa's stories.

Too late.

And right now, I was more concerned with the twinkle in Mama's eye. I knew that twinkle meant trouble for me. What that twinkle actually meant was that Mama had been cooped up in bed too long after having my newest brother and was antsy. A day full of canning strawberry jam would fix that, with me as her helper.

At least, when it was all done and night had fallen, my

fireflies would be waiting for me. It'd be soothing, seeing them blinking and flashing in their disorderly, random way. Little did I know … the fireflies had something special in store for me that night. Something all for me. Something that would change my life forever.

# CHAPTER 3

I should've been in bed. But I snuck outside to the front porch, knowing my beetle friends would arrive soon.

I pulled my knees to my chest, propped my chin on my bony knee, feeling the trickle of summer-time heat trail down my back. Soon, I watched them chatter.

I imagined the silly little things they said:

*Hello!*

*How do you do?*

*Nice evening, is it not?*

Truthfully, heat still hung in the barely-there breeze and I breathed in the humid air, heavy with the day's earlier rain. At least it was cooler outside than in the house. The house got extra hot from the absurd amount of jam Mama and I had cooked today.

"Even with a family as big as ours, we'll never eat this much strawberry jam," I had told her.

Her response had been mostly a noise.

"I could take it down to Ludingtonville, see if anyone there wants to buy some."

Mama had looked up at that. Ludingtonville was named after us: the Ludingtons. It wasn't a town or a city or a village—those had churches and schools—but Ludingtonville was a tiny hamlet on our land, consisting of our two mills, a postal office, a shared stable, and a stretch of homes on either side of a single road, occupied mainly by the families who worked the mills.

"It's right over the hill," I had added, if that was Mama's concern. I knew it was. She didn't like me or my sisters leaving the clearing by ourselves. But Ludingtonville was still on our property. I could walk there in no time. My arms would be plenty tired by the time I got there. Now, if I had a cart and horse ....

But Mama had shaken her head. "You'll get nothing but strange looks if you try selling our goods. Peddling isn't an appropriate occupation for a girl."

I had sighed then.

I sighed now.

I stared into the vast darkness speckled with flashes of light. The only other light illuminated from a single candle at my side. What was beyond our many acres and the trees I saw from Johnny Whitaker's cart on the way to the schoolhouse?

I stretched out my legs and I felt it in my bones that twelve was to be a big year for me. I wasn't sure why, exactly. But feelings didn't always need to be explained. Papa always told me that. Mama was more down-to-earth.

I smiled at the emerging fireflies. There was a blink here, a blink there. I enjoyed guessing where the next light would appear, the activity beginning to tire my brain. I yawned, just as a sound drifted from the woods, the yawn muffling the noise in my ears. It was likely an owl. I stood, a second yawn coming over me. But, before I could turn to go inside, something happened.

Something magical.

The fireflies blinked all at once, in harmony.

Despite the balmy night, my skin erupted with goose bumps. I couldn't believe it. They had done the same thing for Papa, asking him to follow them to safety when he had been on the battlefield.

What were they trying to tell me?

To follow them?

All together, the fireflies flickered again, and again. Each time, it was as if the grouping moved away, closer to the tree line.

Not a single stitch of me was tired any longer.

They blinked, now within the trees.

"Wait," I said and stepped from the stone porch and into the grass, bringing my candle with me. The darkness suddenly felt everywhere. I shuddered as I took a few steps, lengthening and quickening my pace while I strengthened my resolve, and then I was running. The trees loomed closer. Between the trunks, the fireflies were still blinking as one.

My quick movements snuffed out my candle. I paused. The ground's wetness seeped through the soles of my thin slippers.

*Follow us* I imagined them saying. *Don't be scared.*

That was easier said than done. At the tree line, I stopped and peered into the darkness. I knew I shouldn't go into the forest alone at night, not when the nocturnal animals came alive. There were bobcats and coyotes and wolves. I listened. Wolves and coyotes were noisy creatures. Bobcats preferred prey of a smaller size. In my case, I hoped tinier than a twelve-year-old, one who was tall for her age.

The fireflies blinked in unison once more.

*Over here* they seemed to say.

But why?

I drummed my fingers against my nightgown, deliberating. And then I stepped into the trees. I was a tall and brave girl, I reassured myself. And surely, as twigs snapped, branches rustled, and my breath increased, I made enough commotion to scare away anything with a mind to eat me, or at least take a bite out of me. I felt each rock and root beneath my slippers, but I didn't look down to watch my steps. I kept my eyes trained ahead; holding my breath while the bellies of the fireflies went dark, until again, they glowed as one. I heard the noise again. Not an owl, as I had thought. But it also wasn't a growl or a howl.

*This way.*

I followed as quickly as possible, doubt beginning to set in that I'd easily find my way home again. Then, the fireflies stopped moving forward. Maybe ten paces ahead, they hovered, their bellies lighting up every two seconds. It was like a beacon, calling me to the very spot they blinked. *Here* they said.

I obeyed, creeping closer, now being careful with each step I took. Something lay on the ground ahead. Something trembling. Something small, but larger than our dogs. Something closer to the size of one of our goats.

A foal?

The young horse cocked his head at me. His spindly legs were tucked beneath his quaking body. His left ear twitched, then his right.

My mouth hung open. I swung my head in all directions in search of the colt's mother or his owner. But then again … whom had I expected to see in the darkness? Ludingtonville was in the opposite direction. Otherwise, our closest neighbor lived miles away. And while there were horses in both places, Papa never mentioned any of them being pregnant.

Yet here was this baby horse. All alone.

I kneeled.

The day's earlier rain seeped through my nightgown at my knees.

The horse's eyes widened, like he was about to hop to his feet and flee.

"Shh, it's all right, boy," I whispered. "Where's your mama?"

I peered once more into the still and quiet darkness. I realized the fireflies blinked elsewhere now, having said what they needed to say. I was meant to find him here. I gathered that much. But why me?

A thought instantly came to me. Nearly everything that was mine was my family's. There wasn't much that was mine and mine alone. I shared the same brown hair, freckles, and long limbs as Rebecca. Throughout the night, a single quilt was yanked and pulled between my sister and me. Of course, there was the daytime, when I had to fight for Mama's and Papa's attention, when my clothing was borrowed, where I bathed in that shared tub.

But this horse … this horse could be mine.

I could use this horse to take myself to school. Thinking

about that freedom and being Sybil the Unknown and Unexplored puts ants in my pants. But even when we didn't leave the property, we could go for rides, devouring acre after acre of our land.

Who knows where this horse could take me?

He shivered. It wasn't cold, so he must've been scared. I reassured him again, "It'll be all right, boy."

The foal raised his head, moonlight catching a white mark between his eyes. This type of marking, Papa once told me, was called a star.

"Star," I said. "How's that for a name?"

Then, I smiled—because, in that moment, I *had* claimed him as my own. Star was mine. I smiled again. The fireflies had given him to me.

# CHAPTER 4

Now, as I kneeled in front of him in the forest, in the middle of the night, the question was … what was I supposed to *do* with Star?

I knew I wanted him. I had claimed him, but I also wasn't supposed to have him.

Mama and Papa probably thought I was greedy for wanting a third horse, when we already had two. Some families couldn't afford a single one. But we could. We were the only family in the area that owned a sawmill—to make lumber—and also a gristmill—for flour. It made life very comfortable and allowed us to have things like multiple horses.

Yet here was a horse—that needed a home.

My brain immediately decided I needed to hide him. But where? Not here. I'd never leave this poor quivering boy in the forest. There was our barn. Except, Papa woke with the birds and always went straight there. He'd find Star even before I took my first breath of the day. There was also the shared barn in Ludingtonville. It was my best hope for a hiding spot until I could figure out what to do next. There'd be confusion, of course, when he was stumbled upon. But hopefully there wouldn't be much more than that.

"Star," I began. I reached out a hand—slowly, ever so

slowly—and touched his muzzle. He leaned into me and pawed at the ground to shift closer. I bet he smelled strawberry on me.

"That's a good boy," I cooed.

And even while I got the sense he liked me—or at least how I smelled—when I tried to get him to stand by cupping my hand and pretending I had actual food there, he didn't take my fake bait. Smart boy. "Well, I can't carry you," I said, hand on my hip. "You likely weigh more than me. So let's give this another try."

I tapped his belly.

That did the trick. Star hopped to his feet so quickly I took a step back. From there, I began to walk and—fortunately—he followed me like a lost puppy.

The forest was dark without the fireflies, and I moved as quickly as possible, without us falling over branches. The stable was equally dark, the whinny of other horses greeting us. I found an empty stall for Star.

I hated leaving him there. And, as I stroked his nose, I knew this was only a temporary fix. "I'll check on you in the morning, as soon as I can sneak away," I assured him.

On my run home, I immediately missed him trailing behind me. My mind turned like a mill, trying to figure out the next leg of my plan. It would be a disaster if Mama and Papa found him, but maybe I could find the right time to introduce Star to them. I could say I won him, but the next area festival wasn't for another month. I could say he was a gift. But Mama would say a horse was too great of a gift to keep. I could be honest and say I found him.

Honesty.

Yes.

But I could also layer on how he didn't have a mama of his own. And how he was scared. And how he'd taken to me right away. I could say he already saw me as his mama.

What I wouldn't say was how we didn't need Johnny Whitaker anymore to drive us to school. That wouldn't help my case. I'd wait to bring that up.

I fell asleep with how I'd fetch him in the morning dancing through my head. I woke before Rebecca, a rarity. I raced to the window, light coming from the barn. Papa was up. I planned to make a mad dash from the house and toward the barn in Ludingtonville but Mama … she caught me first.

"Sybil? Good," she said, rocking my new baby brother Tertullus. "Can you fetch eggs for breakfast?"

The eggs were fetched.

Then:

"Sybil, the table needs setting."

I set the table.

Then:

"Sybil, can you get breakfast off the stove?"

I did, feeling unnerved at the delays. Star was waiting for me. "Everything is ready," I called to Mama, sidestepping out of the room. Her back was to me.

"Go ahead and eat, sweetie. Rare for you to have first dibs."

"I'm not hungry," I lie.

"Sit," she said. "Eat."

I twisted my lips as I sat and shoveled eggs onto my plate. Mama had made bacon, too.

Papa came in. Rebecca came down. I chewed and swallowed as quickly as I could without choking.

"Girls," Papa said, sitting, "I'm glad you're both here. I wanted to talk to you both."

Oh. I swallowed more carefully. Papa was usually a man of few words, unless he had a story to tell. He loved telling stories. But his eyes looked serious at the moment. I hoped that meant this wouldn't take long. I didn't have long before school and I still needed to race to and from Ludington's stables to check on Star.

Papa began, "I've been asked to help in the cause against the British."

I sat up straighter. "Does that mean you're resigning as a captain for them?"

"No. I'm going to be sly." He waggled his brows. "I'm doing both. But that means I'll be away from home a lot— assisting quietly in any way I can."

He didn't say how, nor was I going to ask. All I knew was that the King of England had recently declared something called the Tea Act. A few days ago I'd overheard Papa say to Mama how it was "unfair to the colonies" and "the final straw." He'd mentioned how we needed "freedom from England."

He added, "I'll be gone days, sometimes weeks at a time. And I'll need you both to do more."

Rebecca had opened her mouth, to say what I couldn't be

sure, but I'd been quicker to respond, saying, "I can help however needed, Papa."

His bright blue eyes focused on me. I sat up straighter in my chair.

"You can read?" Papa asked me.

I nodded.

"And write?"

"And count," I offered.

Papa smiled easily, but it hadn't made his smile any less significant. "Then, I don't believe you need any more schooling, Sybil. I'd like you home full time, starting today."

So much hit my brain at once.

No more school? But that was the only time I ever left our property without my parents. I welcomed it, even with Johnny Whitaker driving me. And I had hoped to stay in school until I could persuade Mama and Papa to overlook how I was a girl and let me apprentice somewhere. But if I began farming full time, the *only* person I'd ever be was Sybil the Farmer's Daughter.

"Sybil," Papa said. He was waiting for me to say, "Yes, sir."

Nobody ever questioned Papa. It was always "Yes, sir." "No, sir." "How high, sir?"

I bet I could jump extra high on Star's back, once he was bigger and I was able to ride him. But first, I had to get to that horse.

That horse ....

That horse … was running toward our house.

Over Papa's shoulder, I saw Star clear as day out through the window.

I remembered myself. "Yes, sir. I'll gladly direct the servants and assist with the planting."

Then my eyes flicked back to the window.

"Good. We should go over the planting schedule."

"I know it," I said quickly. I licked my lips. "Snap beans, winter squash, sweet corn, and pumpkins will be planted next week."

The asparagus, beets, potatoes, and carrots were already in the ground.

Star was almost here, coming straight for the house. And, oh my goodness, there was Johnny Whitaker emerging from the trees. Was he chasing after Star? This was turning into a real pickle.

My feet danced beneath the table. I needed this conversation to end. I needed to get outside. But my sister chimed in, "I'd like to help, too."

I heard in Rebecca's voice that she didn't like that Papa had only spoken to me so far.

"I'll be relying on you both," Papa said. "Both of you, as the two oldest, to help Mama keep the house. She already does too much."

"Yes, sir," I said mechanically. Rebecca said it with more enthusiasm.

"But Rebecca," Papa said. "You can remain in school."

My breath hitched.

Star was at the window. His nose was pressed against it.

Rebecca gasped, and I kicked her beneath the table. My sister didn't even try to hide the fact I kicked her. "Ow!" Her head snapped in my direction.

I focused on Papa. His brows furrowed. Then, I couldn't help it, my gaze flicked to the window again.

"Sybil?"

My strange behavior had been noticed. Papa turned in his chair, finding Star's head only feet away behind the glass. "What on earth?"

# CHAPTER 5

"Whose horse is that? Papa asked. "Abigail!" he called to Mama.

She came running. "What is it? I just got Tertullus down for a nap."

Papa nodded toward Star.

Mama cocked her head. "Don't see a random horse standing at the window every day." But then, "Is that Johnny running this way? Where's his cart?"

I kept my mouth closed as Papa went outside, but better believe I was right behind him. Better believe my presence also brought Star straight to me when he saw me, which I should've expected by the fact he showed up at my house with his nose pressed against the window, looking for me. Horses had a unique ability of always finding their way home. I liked that I was already his home.

My smile was instant, even as I felt all eyes on me.

Mama said, drawing out my name, "Sybil?"

Honesty, I reminded myself. Though, succinct honesty was probably the best idea. "I found him and—"

"No, I found him," Johnny Whitaker interrupted. "I went to feed Rosemary to get her ready to pick up your girls, but I noticed the top of a head in a stall that's normally empty. I found the horse, but when I opened the stall to get a better look at him, he took off!"

I put a hand on my hip. "And who do you think put Star in that stall?"

"Star?" Johnny Whitaker said. "I didn't know he had a name."

Papa said, "The name is of little importance. How ... when ... did you put that horse in the barn?"

"In Ludingtonville," Mama added with a frown.

My sister hadn't yet said a word, but she fought a smile. Rebecca was enjoying Mama and Papa acting surly with me.

"I found him last night when I couldn't sleep. I was worried you wouldn't let me keep him, so I put him in the barn down at the hamlet until I could figure out what to do."

"What you mean is that you hid the horse from us?" Mama said.

I grimaced. I did, but it sounded really bad. "I'm sorry," I said. "But can I keep him? He likes me. He thinks I'm his mama."

"He ran here, Johnny?" Papa asked. "Straight here?"

Johnny Whitaker shook his head. "Like he knew the way. He's a fast thing, especially for a foal."

"Papa," I said. "Papa, the fireflies led me to Star."

Mama sighed in annoyance. "Not that story again."

But I'd already gotten Papa's attention. Papa loved those fireflies. He believed in them, too. "I guess it wouldn't be the end of the world to have another horse around the farm."

"Henry!" Mama said.

I excitedly rolled onto my tiptoes.

"You can keep him, Sybil," Papa said. "He'll be helpful

with all your extra responsibility, *if* no one comes to claim him."

That stole some of my excitement. Star could've been anyone's. I knew Papa hoped he didn't belong to a Loyalist. They hadn't come to scare us again, now that Papa was technically a British captain. But Papa also wouldn't want any unwanted attention, especially now that he had just told us he'd be doing hush-hush things against the British.

It turned my stomach, Papa playing both sides and also how he had freedom on the brain. The other day when Papa and Mama had been talking about it, Mama had hissed back, "Freedom comes at a cost. My uncle. My cousin. Both of them dead."

That turned my stomach, too. Mama didn't talk about it much, but she'd been referring to the French and Indian War. Papa had been only fifteen, Mama even younger. She'd seen and heard enough to know she never wanted to witness war again.

The chance of Papa in a battle one day scared me, but right now I could only think about what was right in front of me. My boy.

We each went our own ways, with Johnny Whitaker home to get Rosemary, Rebecca inside to get changed for school, Mama to the pump for water, Papa into town for his first secret meeting, and me to the barn with Star.

I groomed him, enjoying each long brush down his back, then grudgingly moved on to more chores. Lots of them, being I was home full time now. But every time I had a view of our long gravel drive, I peered down it, waiting to see if a horseless man wanted to take mine.

# CHAPTER 6

No one came to claim Star.

He was mine.

All mine.

"Come on, boy," I said, a few days later.

Under the intensity of the midday sun, I ran beside Star, the ties of my bonnet loosening, the grass brushing against my long skirt, nearly tripping over my feet because I was excited to have him.

Rebecca and Mary were at school. My other siblings old enough to tumble were doing so elsewhere with the dogs. Papa was in town, meeting again with other important men. Mama saw to the house, when Tertullus wasn't wailing to be fed. The servants were busy with their daily routines. I'd completed all my morning chores and my afternoon ones were set to begin soon. But for now, it was just Star and me. We'd quickly fallen into a habit of training together before dusk, but I snuck in extra time whenever I could.

I guessed Star to be at least six months old, because when Nellie—that'd be one of our cows—dripped milk from her udders, Star showed no signs of wanting to drink. Papa said foals weaned from their mamas by half a year old.

I also counted his height to be twelve hands, from the ground to his shoulders. But if you added on Star's neck and head, he was around my height, just over five feet. Now, side-by-side, we ran, his head right next to mine.

From the corner of his eye, I felt Star watching me.

My heart swelled.

It was my job to teach him, especially since he didn't have a horse mama to learn from. Rebecca wanted to train him, too, but I insisted that it'd only confuse him. She grumbled. I shrugged. Papa *had* said I could keep him for myself. And I'd come to the conclusion that it was why the fireflies brought me to Star, so that I could have something all my own.

He couldn't be ridden yet. Not for a while. But earlier today I had put a saddle on him, so he could get a feel for it. He instantly shook, like a dog getting the rain off. It'd be new for both of us. We'd learn it together.

"Got no problem running, though, do you, Star?" I asked him, my breath growing ragged as we ran next to each other. At the tree line, I slowed us to a walk, and then took a few quick steps, so I was in front. "Follow me, boy."

His nose bumped my back. I stopped, turned, and lightly pressed my palm over his chest. Star took a step back. I smiled; pleased he listened to my silent command to give me some room. Mama once said, "If you give your brothers an inch, they'll take a mile." Horses were like that, too.

I led Star through the trees, walking us right toward fallen tree limbs. I stepped over. Star stepped over.

"Good boy," I cooed.

It was part of his training. When he was bigger, he'd learn to jump them. I looked back, making sure I could still see the house. Mama's rule.

"Say," I asked him, "since I don't know your exact birthday, how about we share mine?" April fifth. Funny, sharing with my sisters and brothers felt like getting caught in a prickly bush. But sharing with Star felt different. *Special*. I didn't mind sharing a birthday with him one bit.

∾

That was what we did, we shared birthdays. And, we aged together. Him one, me thirteen. Him two, me fourteen. Now Star was three and I was fifteen. And as we approached the middle of 1776, my fears of Papa having to fight one day in a battle felt all too real.

He hadn't yet. But a full-blown war between the colonies and England began last year up north. The story of how it all started was now a legend, spread from one supper table to another.

"England's General Gage thought himself a sneak," Papa said around ours, beginning his story with an excited pitch to his voice. "Just not a very good one." Papa smirked. "Gage ordered the King's troops who were quartering in Boston to seize our gunpowder in Concord, and on the way, stop in Lexington to arrest our Colonial leaders—Samuel Adams and John Hancock. Only, it didn't go as Gage expected." Papa forked a potato and smiled as he chewed. "We had spies."

I held my breath, and envisioned the spies dressed in all black to better fade into the night or perchance the men were disguised in the uniform of the British. Listening. Plotting. Divulging the King's secrets back to our Colonial leaders. It was all very exhilarating. Though, I was certain also very dangerous.

Papa said, "Paul Revere, one of our illustrious spies, discovered that the British troops had conspired to leave Boston that night for Lexington. Atop a church in the bell tower, Revere hung two lanterns."

I wasn't privy to what that meant, the hanging of those lanterns. And, I didn't dare disrupt Papa's retelling. To my relief, he explained, "It was a signal, you see. Two lanterns meant the British planned to leave Boston by sea. One light meant they planned to march entirely by land."

By sea they went, across the Charles River. Mr. Revere did the same. His task was to cross the waters then travel to Lexington on horseback to warn Mr. Adams and Mr. Hancock that the British were planning an ambush.

Papa's voice held a boastful tone. "In his tiny rowboat, Revere sailed right past the British Warship *HMS Somerset*."

And then Mr. Revere found a horse and was on his way. Galloping through the countryside. Narrowly escaping capture by a British patrol. Calling to the militiamen, asleep in their houses, that the British troops were coming. His words were meant to rouse them, so they could face the British troops at Lexington.

I shivered at the thought … of the threat of capture, of riding through the fields and woods with only the moonlight to guide me, of putting myself at greater risk by calling out an alert. I peered beyond Papa and out the window. I only saw the outline of Star's barn. It was too dark for details. How did Mr. Revere know where to go, especially after changing his course after his near capture? How his heart must've raced.

And then, how proud and relieved he must've been when he successfully warned Mr. Adams and Mr. Hancock. He could've stopped, but Mr. Revere was determined to warn those in Concord, too. He set off, once more on horseback, with Mr. William Dawes. Along the way, Dr. Samuel Prescott joined them.

"The second leg of Revere's journey proved more harrowing," Papa said. "Revere traveled with the two men until … he was captured."

I gasped, especially at the simplicity of Papa's delivery, and I couldn't help but ask, "Did they hang him?" This happened to spies. Johnny Whitaker mentioned it once. But I tried to forget ever hearing it. "And what of the other two men?"

"Dawes and Prescott eluded capture and delivered the news. And, by the grace of God, the British only took Revere's horse before releasing him."

I set down my fork, which I'd held in the air the entire time Papa told the story. Just listening to the tale had exhausted me. I felt exhausted for Mr. Paul Revere, too. But I also felt scared that something similar could happen to Papa, now that he was a known Patriot. A rebel.

Because of Mr. Paul Revere, our troops were able to stop an ambush by the British. That was when the first shot of the war was fired. After that, Papa was done playing both sides.

*Traitor!* I sometimes heard in my head, goose bumps erupting on my skin each time. And sometimes, when Mama thought no one was watching, I caught her wringing her hands.

# CHAPTER 7

The next day, Johnny Whitaker returned my sisters and brothers from school, then moseyed over toward where I was checking the crops for weeds, bugs, disease, or ponding.

"Star seems to be doing well," he remarked.

My boy was doing great. I'd been riding him for a while now, Star no longer afraid of the saddle. In fact, Star was currently watching me from the pastures. He wanted to go for a ride.

"How about a ride?" Johnny Whitaker asked, as if he could read my boy's mind.

I examined a leaf. "I've only ever taken him out."

"I meant I could go with you."

I twisted my lips. I wasn't one to say no to a ride. I'd just never said yes to someone riding with me before. Rebecca had asked.

It was hot, though. Real hot under this August sun. We could do a lap or two around the clearing for a slight breeze. "I'll get him ready."

When I returned with Star, already on his back, Johnny Whitaker had a smile on his face. "You don't ride sidesaddle?"

"We don't own a side saddle. So, no."

"Doesn't your dress make it harder?"

"Not really." Though, I admitted to myself I wouldn't mind trying pants.

I added, "Papa told me Catherine the Great rides with a leg on either side. And if it's good enough for a great, then it's good enough for me."

"Then I shall call you Sybil the Great." He reached for the reins, as if he assumed I'd scoot behind the saddle and he'd ride in front. I shook my head. "Get behind me if you want to come, Johnny Whitaker."

"But—"

I raised my eyebrows at him.

"Fine," he grumbled.

He climbed up, but kept his hands to himself. I was fine and dandy about that. "The wind gets you more up here, doesn't it?"

I closed my eyes, feeling the air on my skin. It was refreshing. But the darkness of my eyelids sparked the memory of Papa's story from last night, and how Mr. Paul Revere had courageously ridden through the night. "Did you hear the story of Mr. Revere yet?"

"I did. They were talking about it in the stables."

"He was so brave to do that. Our colonists won that first battle, too. Mr. Revere had a big hand in that. Spying on the British, galloping through the night, putting himself at risk—"

"Don't tell me you're in a dizzy for him?"

"I'm not. It's only that I couldn't imagine doing that. I'm impressed. I'm allowed to be impressed."

"But you're a girl."

"Oh am I?"

"And now you're a wiseacre, huh?" I heard the laugh in his voice. "I only mean to say that Revere seems like an odd hero for a girl to have."

"Enlighten me, Johnny Whitaker, who should I have as a hero then?"

He leaned forward and around me the best he could to see me better. "How come you're always using my full name? It makes me feel like I'm in trouble."

I shrugged without turning my head to meet his gaze. I wanted to get back to my hero question. I asked again, "Who should my hero be?"

"Another woman? You're not going to grow up to be Revere, are you? You don't even wear pants."

"Very funny." But really, it was my insides that felt funny. I didn't realize it was weird for me to want to be brave or daring or courageous like a man was. I often looked up to Papa. And hadn't Papa thought Catherine the Great was great enough to model after? Though, I realized, I was a girl modeling after another woman. Papa hadn't said, "His Excellency General Washington rides astride, so it'd be excellent for you to do the same, Sybil."

Johnny Whitaker went on. "Shouldn't your mama be your hero? Besides, she's brave, too, in her own way."

"Not about this war. She hates it."

Ever since those first shots, there'd been sieges, and the

seizing of forts, and no fewer than fifteen battles. Most of those battles had been farther north or had involved our Southern Army. But now, the battles had come to New York and Papa was no longer doing secret stuff. He joined the Colonial military and had risen through the ranks to a colonel. He even was assigned his own regiment and troops to lead: a lot of them, who needed a place to congregate and wait until they were called upon by Papa or, more importantly, by His Excellency General George Washington himself. That meant an encampment, right on our property, so Papa could get there quickly.

Johnny Whitaker said, "Bet your mama isn't happy about the troops camping on your land."

"Not one bit."

"Have you seen it?"

"Seen what?"

"The camp."

I shook my head. "Mama doesn't like me going far from the house."

"I can tell. We're practically doing circles. Is she afraid of the Cowboys?"

The Cowboys. They were an outlaw group, loyal to the Loyalists.

"I wouldn't say afraid," I said, "but Papa's troops get called often to deal with them."

The Cowboys were trouble. They jingled cowbells to lure farmers, making them think one of their cows had gotten stuck in a thicket. Then they'd jump out and rob the farmers. They'd steal their horses and cattle, and then they'd sell the livestock to the British.

"Well, if we hear any cowbells, we'll turn back. What do you say? Let's go see your papa's camp. I'm curious. My papa's there now, too."

I shook my head. "You go see it and your papa on your own time. I still have chores to do."

"Are you seriously going to tell me you're not curious, too?"

Maybe I was.

"Come on," he pestered, even using both hands to shake me in front of him on Star. "In a year, I'll be enlisting. I want to see what I'm in for."

I huffed at that. As a girl, enlisting was something else I wouldn't be allowed to do. If I'm stuck on this farm forever, never allowed to go far from the house, this could be my only opportunity to see an encampment. We were around the back of the house. I looked over my shoulder. Mama or Papa wasn't anywhere to be seen. Rebecca's voice drifted from around the house's front.

I steered Star in the direction of Papa's camp.

I stopped us well away from it. Johnny Whitaker wanted to go closer, but Mama would have my hide if she knew I was even this close.

"Can't tell which one is my pa," he said.

Me neither. At this distance, it wasn't much to see: tents, log cabins, pits for fire, men walking about like ants.

But I saw it and that made me smile, until I thought about how girls weren't allowed down there, even though I could do everything those men could do. In fact, I probably cooked better, with all my practice.

I regripped Star's reins. "Well, we best get back."

On our way home, I leaned onto Star's neck to avoid a branch. Johnny Whitaker leaned into me, heavier than I thought he'd be. Star's body was hot. I hadn't noticed how low the sun had fallen. The late summer's daylight hours were shorter each day. Mama would be looking for me. I urged Star to increase his pace, applying pressure with my legs. He responded. We emerged at the crest of a rolling hill. My house wasn't far off.

"You better tell my mama this was your idea if she hollers—"

I caught the sound of men's voices, more easily carried in the cooling air. I stopped Star.

"You hear that?" I asked Johnny Whitaker.

"Yeah."

I faced Star toward the voices, the deep tones coming from the opposite direction of Papa's troops. We listened, Star's ears flicking back and forth. Then he snorted.

That got me nervous.

A high-pitched whinny meant *where are you?*

A breathy nicker meant *look at me!*

A loud snort meant *danger?*

"He just snorted," I said to Johnny Whitaker.

"Is that a bad sign?"

"It's not good." Nerves pricked my voice.

"Sounds really close."

I nodded. The words *Lets go, boy* were on the tip of my tongue. I could … I should … follow those words with a pull of a rein toward home, not that Star would even need that tug.

But this afternoon shook me up. I wanted to be brave— even if I was a girl.

"Let's go see," I said and instead of leading Star toward home, I directed him toward the men. I could be—and would be—more than Sybil the Farmer's Daughter.

# CHAPTER 8

Atop Star, Johnny Whitaker and I peered down into a valley. Star's feet stomped and I stroked his neck in a calming manner. The field below us was vast, with so many dwarf trees that they formed a thicket. Few leaves covered the trees, and the lack of foliage left the men observable, where they squatted and sat beneath the intertwining branches.

Hiding?

On our land? I couldn't be sure if we owned it. There wasn't a fence that surrounded the entirety of our two hundred and twenty-nine acres, nor had I been allowed to set foot on the half of it. I certainly wouldn't have had a reason to traipse through such a scrub oak field.

But it appeared these men did have a reason—whatever that may've been. I prayed it wasn't to steal our cattle or destroy our crops. I had worked really hard on those plants.

The thing was, if I could see them, they could see Johnny Whitaker and me.

"Get off," I whispered to him.

He did, and I slipped off Star's back too, dropped the reins, and pushed gently on Star's chest. Star responded, taking awkward steps backward until he was out of sight. Johnny Whitaker sidled behind a nearby tree and I joined him. There, I fought to steady my racing heart and watched the men.

"Cowboys?" Johnny Whitaker mouthed to me.

"Hope not."

But if not them, then who?

I didn't want to answer that question, but I knew in my gut that these men could've been here because of Papa, because they saw him as a traitor once again.

They were mainly motionless, save for a scratch here and a man repositioning there. They spoke in deep voices I couldn't make out. Someone coughed. Then, a man began to move about, bending to talk to a handful of others. He twisted his body to maneuver between the scrub trees, and then spoke to another grouping.

I squinted, leaning closer, and realized I recognized the man. Mr. Nickerson, Nicholson, Nicklaus? Oh, pooh! What was his name?

"I know him," I whispered to Johnny Whitaker. "That one talking." I was sure I'd seen the man before. I searched my brain. "He dined at our table, as a guest of Papa's."

"He must be a rebel then like us."

"They did talk about the cause with great enthusiasm."

I circled my lips and blew out a silent breath. They weren't Cowboys. They weren't here for Papa.

That was a relief.

But what on earth was he and the other men doing here?

"You going to tell your Papa you saw him?"

I toed the dirt, thinking. "I don't know. That'd mean

admitting I was all the way out here."

"Sybil, you truly are a rebel."

"Quiet," I said to quiet him. Darkness began to steal the men's faces. "If we don't get back soon, I'll be in trouble for being late to supper."

I started to turn, but motion stopped me. The men were emerging from beneath the small trees, like insects breaking free from a hive. The men's clothing was ordinary and dark. But then a splash of color—red and blue—caught my eye. It was a flag.

But it wasn't our flag I saw—with thirteen stars to align with our thirteen colonies. It was Britain's flag—with a large red cross. My breath hitched. They may have not have been Cowboys, but I was still very wrong. These men were not fellow rebels like Papa. They were rivals. They were Loyalists. They *could* have been here for Papa.

I didn't matter how much trouble I could've gotten in for being so far from the house. I had to get home to warn Papa. *Now.*

# CHAPTER 9

I stumbled backward until I reached Star and pulled myself onto his back. Johnny Whitaker was behind me a second later.

It took me two tries to get a firm grip on the reins.

Papa had made himself a target.

A traitor-sized target, who now also led troops against them.

Papa was a threat twice over. Did these Loyalists mean to ransack our farm, go after his men, or maybe scare Papa into abandoning his war efforts?

"Ho," I breathed into Star's neck.

Warning Papa was all that mattered now.

Star's footfalls banged in my head like gunfire.

As we approached my house, I told Johnny Whitaker to get ready.

"For what?"

I slowed Star, nearly to a stop, when I called to him, "Jump off!"

In his hurry, he all but fell off my horse and I thrust myself from Star's back. The ground met me hard and my legs gave out. On my knees, I saw the glow of many, many candles beyond our windows. Mama loved their flickering light. She'd put candles on top of candles if it worked that way. It didn't, but they were everywhere throughout the house. Behind the curtains, silhouettes moved about, in the parlor, the sitting and weaving rooms, and the kitchen. Those rooms all faced the house's front. With a family as large as ours, it looked like a small army.

I climbed to my feet again, and ran, guessing Papa to be one of the silhouettes in the parlor. There, I breathlessly told him what—or rather who—I saw.

Within minutes, Papa saddled Pepper.

"While I'm away ..." Papa began. The whole family was outside for his send off. Everyone looked nervous. I was no different. Johnny Whitaker was still there. So was Star. Rosemary, too. "While I'm away, Johnny, would you keep an eye on the lands? Just like you did tonight? Can you ride Rosemary?"

My mouth dropped open.

Johnny Whitaker glanced at me. "Rosemary can be ridden. But, sir, it was Sybil's idea. I'd like it if she could join me with Star."

Papa thought on it a moment. A moment was all he had. "Very well. The two of you will patrol."

Then Papa was gone, racing toward his regiment's camp.

Mama didn't have a moment to object. But she did pin me in place with her eyes. "Your idea, huh? Hope it's your idea to get up early for the next week to milk Nellie, too."

"Yes, ma'am."

Mama started ushering my brothers and sisters inside like they were chickens.

I loitered on our gravel drive, Johnny Whitaker next to me. I asked him, "Are you going to help me with the milking, too?"

"Don't make me lie to you."

I shook my head and stared into the darkness long after Papa had disappeared. Star nudged my arm.

"Good boy," I said to him.

"Thanks," Johnny Whitaker said impishly.

I let a smile creep onto my face. But even as my outsides smiled, my insides were churning with unease. I'd made guesses, but I wondered what those men truly wanted, what they were after, what dangers it could've meant for Papa. They weren't far from my home. Had they meant to come here, like they had before?

I searched the darkening night for fireflies, but there was none to be found to help me answer that question. I was left with only my thoughts. Before, with the nearby battles and the nearby outlaw groups, I understood that the war had made its way to New York. That unsettled Mama enough, especially with Papa and his men being called upon so often. But now the goings-on were closer than ever. Mere minutes as opposed to many miles. At the realization, I both tired and shuddered.

# CHAPTER 10

For once, while I waited for Papa's return, I was happy to have endless amounts of farm work to distract me from worrying about him. I even looked forward to Johnny Whitaker arriving with his horse and cart. I think he did, too. We'd been doing our afternoon ride for weeks now, so long that the fireflies went underground, leaving me anxious without their nightly chatter. I missed them. I missed Papa. But I still believed that if I needed my beetle friends, they'd be there for me miraculously.

After unloading my siblings, Johnny Whitaker was quick to remove the cart from Rosemary. Then, we were off to patrol. This afternoon I noticed how Rebecca lingered, watching us go until Mama called for her.

"Think our papas will be back soon?" I asked Johnny Whitaker. We rode side by side.

Johnny Whitaker shrugged. "Not like mine will actually be back. He'll just go back to the camp. I had to give up my apprenticeship to do my pa's work at the mill."

"I'm sorry," I said, meaning it.

"Me, too. But I'd have to give it up when I turn sixteen anyway."

We were both born in April, only a few days apart, in fact. Here I thought I was limited, as a girl. But being a boy during this war meant limitations, too. I was curious what going to war would be like, beyond the stories I'd been told. "My papa told me he had to eat bark before."

Johnny Whitaker grimaced.

"During the French and Indian War, their camp ran short on food. So they ate bark from birch trees and juniper berries."

"How was it?"

I thought on it. "You know what, he never said."

"Try it then. Tell me what it tastes like."

"Me?"

He nodded.

"Only if you do it, too."

We were quick to find berries. Bark was everywhere. I swore Star looked at me like I'd lost my mind when I placed both in my mouth.

It wasn't good.

But what had I expected?

"I think I got a bug with mine." Johnny Whitaker stuck out his tongue, covered in brown disgustingness.

I laughed. "Maybe we're not cut out for war life."

But while we rode on, continuing the surveying of my property for anybody who wasn't supposed to be there, Mr. Revere slipped into my thoughts. I urged Star faster. I pretended we had another urgent message to deliver and that the British could be anywhere. Johnny Whitaker shouted, "Hey!" then quickly caught up. "What was that?" he asked.

But I didn't want to answer him. I felt foolish mentioning

my so-called hero again. "It's getting dark," I said instead.

The next day, I distracted myself with a newfangled invention from Mr. Thomas Jefferson: a swivel chair. I sat in front of the handloom in our weaving room and gave myself a whirl, allowing the contraption's motion to stop on its own. How handy it was. One second I was facing the loom, then the next the spinning wheel. Almost like hocus-pocus. The invention was brilliancy, and I swiveled whenever and wherever possible. It made making clothes almost bearable.

"You'll never get done with all your dilly-dallying," Rebecca said, nearly finished with her sewing.

I shrugged. Another whirl sent me facing the wide window in our weaving room. Outside, Star grazed. A beautiful creature he was, sorrel in color, matching the changing leaves, and with that white starburst I loved above his eyes. He looked up, chewing idly, then in my direction. Of course he did. Our brains were tethered together, and I knew what he was thinking: *Was it time for our daily ride?*

I sighed, wishing I were anywhere but in the sewing room. Rebecca informed me she was done, pride in her voice. She left, missing my eye roll, and I moved on to patching one of Papa's pants, using my chair to swivel to reach the precut fabric square. I loved this chair.

After the patch was in place, I reluctantly stood to shake out Papa's pants.

I wondered … I wondered what it'd be like to try them on. I blamed Johnny Whitaker for putting the thought there, when he'd asked me before about riding Star while in a dress.

I looked left. I looked right. I didn't see anyone, except Star. He still watched me.

I climbed into Papa's pants, pulling them up. His knee breeches went well below my knees. They fell right off my hips. Really, they billowed all around me.

I felt ridiculous, with how big they were. But I didn't have any brothers big enough to try on their pants; the oldest, Archibald, was nine. And there was no chance I was going to ask Johnny Whitaker to take off his breeches. I blushed at the thought, at his reaction, and anything having to do with Johnny Whitaker standing there in nothing but his stockings and long shirt.

A noise startled me. I dropped Papa's pants. Someone was coming and I was about to get caught with Papa's pants around my ankles.

I kicked out of them, losing my balance and falling to the floor. I made a thump. I lay there for a moment, stunned, my elbow aching, and I decided wearing a dress suited me just fine. That was when I heard Papa's voice.

Papa! He was the cause of the noise! He was back!

It was enough to make me forget I was on the floor. Un-moving, I listened to the deep, familiar tones of his voice. He was telling Mama how General Washington needed him further—and with haste. Papa's efforts had originally begun with him seeing to those squatting on our land—the ones I had told him about—but then he and his men had been called to a battle in Long Island. Only, Papa never wrote to tell us this, so we'd spent the time worrying, Mama especially.

Papa's boots knocked against the hardwoods seconds later as he left the kitchen and began to pass through the weaving room. Papa went right by me. Then his brow furrowed. He turned back.

"Sybil? What are you doing down there?"

"Tripped," I said. It was the truth.

"Are those my pants?"

I nodded.

"Excellent. I need a fresh pair. Also, I must thank you, Sybil, for your intelligence."

My lips parted but were quick to form a smile. I stood, my chin a little higher than usual. Papa had said intelligence, not as in my wits—though I thought I was a rather smart girl, if I do say so myself—but *intelligence* as in the information I'd provided. Helpful information.

"Without you," Papa said, "those men would've attacked my encampment." He smiled at me as Mama appeared from the kitchen, her knuckles white as she clutched her apron.

Papa nodded for me to follow him. In quick sentences, while gathering his necessities, he told us about the man I'd seen on our land. He *had* sat at our table as a Patriot, before he switched sides. With the information Johnny Whitaker and I provided—who, where, how many—Papa and his troops had surrounded them. The struggle had been severe, but Papa and his men were victorious. The Loyalists now sat in a prison.

And the man who'd once sat at our table would've been hanged, if Papa hadn't stepped in and pleaded on his behalf. He'd been spared.

This all made me happy. It did. But Papa's success also made me want to turn my knuckles as white as Mama's. Papa was already considered a traitor. He was known as a leader. Now, he was also a saboteur. I once thought of Papa as a double threat. Was he now a threat three times over? Because of my intelligence?

I twisted my lips as Papa went on. After defeating those men, Papa explained how he was sent to help with the battle at Long Island. It hadn't gone well. We'd lost, and Papa was eager to face the British again.

Rebecca joined us at some point during Papa's recounting. Her mouth turned down as she listened and at how Papa rustled my braids, thanking me again.

With that, Papa rode off on Pepper, promising Mama he'd write us this time while he was away. In the days that followed, while I gathered pumpkins or picked the last of the season's apples, I noticed Rebecca trying to saddle Jasper. But the old boy hadn't ever been ridden before. He was a field horse. Judging by his response, he wished to stay that way, no matter how hard Rebecca wanted to ride him. What did she want to do? Join Johnny Whitaker and me on our scouting rides so she could impress Papa, too?

Mama got her way and Papa wrote us daily, but his letters weren't delivered daily. Some afternoons we received nothing, making the entire family even hungrier for his words. If there were a way to deliver information in an instant, it'd be another form of magic. Then a few days later we'd receive a flurry of news.

On one of those days, Mama read triumphantly how General Washington showed Papa great favor. How? He hadn't said, but we all sang merrily that night, knowing Papa was well and doing well.

The downside was how Papa continued to be needed, long enough where the holidays were upon us. Separated by too many miles, I whispered into the wind Happy Christmas to Papa, then a week later I silently wished him a Happy New Year as 1776 turned to 1777.

Papa's letters held great excitement in January as he told us how General Washington had had two great triumphs that were two great turning points. One at Trenton. Another in Princeton.

His latest letter, however, was a present ripe for the holiday season. General Washington was to winter in Morristown and Papa … Papa was to return home.

Mama decided on a feast, and as night began to fall, we lined up by age at the windows to wait. I drummed my fingers against the windowsill. Rebecca and Mary did the same. Archibald, Henry, Derick, and Tertullus were next, jostling shoulders and letting out high-pitched noises. Mama tapped her foot while holding Little Abigail, who was my newest of siblings, nearly a year old. She made eight of us. Three girls. Then four boys. Now another girl. I was taking bets for another girl next.

Finally, Papa arrived on Pepper.

Our reunion was a happy one, but Papa seemed to hold an extra twinkle of excitement in his eyes as we ate and as the night grew longer.

"What is it, Papa?" I asked, after Mama had herded my younger siblings upstairs for bed and returned to the table. Only Rebecca, Papa, Mama, and me remained sitting there.

His response filled me with a thrill but also with trepidation.

"General Washington has named me one of his aides," he said first. Mama gasped at the great honor. Then she caught herself, remembering how she was a peacemaker and didn't support the war. She closed her mouth, but Papa wasn't done yet. "He'll be spending the winter at a camp in Morristown, but he asked me to join him in May. Until then," he said, "His Excellency wishes for me to do something secretive."

Papa paused, letting the anticipation build. Then he whispered, "He wants me to begin to build a secret ring of spies."

A spy ring? Such a thing existed only in stories, not in real life. Both excitement and apprehension made my question sound more like a croak, as I asked, "Where are you going to build your secret spy ring?"

Papa lifted a brow, looking mischievous. "Right here."

# CHAPTER 11

A spy ring here? "In our home?"

Papa nodded and then he eyed me, watching for my reaction. "The thing is … I won't be able to do it alone. Not with His Excellency also wanting me to take meetings, march with my men when there's a need and such. I'll need your help, Sybil."

My help—forming a secret ring of spies? And, my reaction, I was ashamed to admit, was a protective hand around my neck. When spies were caught, spies were hung.

Papa went on. "I'll need your help, too, Rebecca."

"Really?" Rebecca said, leaning forward, her blouse nearly into her supper plate, where juices and sauce still remained.

My sister's eagerness had me lowering my hand from my neck to my lap. I pointed out, "But Rebecca is at school during the day."

"Not anymore," he said. "As I said, Rebecca will be needed here. Both of you are to help, together."

I felt Rebecca's eyes on me, surely smug that Papa needed her, too. I moved my focus to Mama. I was surprised she hadn't spoken yet. But then she licked her lips. "Henry," she said in her low voice, her voice that meant she wasn't happy. "Perhaps we could talk about this later?"

"I've been given my orders, Abigail, and I'll need help

from the girls if this is to be a success."

I asked, "How are we going to help?" before Mama could get another word in.

"General Washington has asked me to choose the spies, to direct them, and"—his gaze flicked to Mama—"when needed, to hide them in our home."

"Henry," Mama said again in that same low tone.

He reached across our big oak table to cover her hand with his. "Without spies, this war would likely have ended last month in Trenton, the victory going to the King of England. But General Washington is quite fond of special agents. Girls," he said, his face and voice growing more animated, "General Washington was brilliant. Clever. Sharp. Our leader is no booby."

"What'd he do, Papa?" Rebecca asked. She'd already been on the edge of her seat.

Now I was, too. "Yeah, Papa, what did he do?"

"The General knows the British are better trained. You put their men against our men in an open field and"—Papa flapped his lips like Star did when thunder cracked in the sky—"the results aren't in our favor. As it was, the General and our militia had suffered one defeat after another and retreated into Pennsylvania. Across the Delaware River, in Trenton, the British were planning their attack. General Washington knew our militia wouldn't stand a chance if that happened. So that brilliant, clever man planted a spy, a Mr. John Honeyman." Papa wagged a finger at us. "Now, this is where the story gets exciting. Honeyman used to be loyal to the British, so when he showed up in Trenton, they thought he still was. He gathered as much information as he could about the British's attack plans, then he wandered off into the woods where he was conveniently *captured*."

The smile grew on my face. "Captured by us, you mean? Like it was part of General Washington's plan all along?"

Papa drew out his response, "Ex-act-ly. Honeyman told General Washington everything he'd learned. Then, who can guess what happened next?"

I wouldn't call Mama's expression merry, but the deep stress line that had been between her eyes had softened. "General Washington attacked," she said. "We know he won at Trenton."

Papa smiled at Mama. "He did. He won indeed. But he didn't attack yet. You see, General Washington is fond of spies, like I said, but also something called *misinformation*—the art of planting fake information. Honeyman 'escaped' and high-tailed it back to the British." Papa pantomimed Mr. Honeyman in the silliest of voices, as if he were a clown instead of a soldier, "The Colonists are weak. The Colonists are tired. The Colonists are disorganized. The Colonists couldn't possibly attack." Papa's voice returned to normal. "But an attack—an *unexpected* attack—is exactly what General Washington intended to do. The British believed Honeyman's misinformation and, secretly, General Washington moved his troops across the icy Delaware River in the middle of the night. As dawn arrived, so did our militia. They took Trenton by surprise, without a single fatality. And that, my dear family, is how spies win wars."

Papa raised his drinking glass an inch then slammed the cup back down. "We'll begin in the morning."

⌘

We'd begin a spy ring in the morning. I couldn't sleep. Next to me, Rebecca was sleeping soundly. But no, not me. The word *spy* kept dancing through my mind.

*Spy* and *danger* and how *spies win wars*.

I was to have a hand in this war, more than simply telling Papa that Loyalists were squatting on our land. Soon, there would be spies sharing my very own roof.

I knew Mama didn't like that.

Mama and Papa's bedroom was beneath mine.

The argument they were having grew louder, and louder.

I crept from my bed, careful to shift my weight slowly so I didn't wake Rebecca. My bare feet made barely a sound against the floors. Although the hardwoods were always cold, this January they were particularly cold.

I crossed my arms as I tiptoed, as much for warmth, but also so I didn't mistakenly reach out and knock over a vase or bump a frame on the wall. Once downstairs, I crept as close to the wall as possible, where the floorboards didn't creak, and gingerly approached my parent's bedroom door. There, I pressed my ear to the wood. It felt dishonorable, to spy in this way. Spies, in general, were considered dishonorable, since their goal was to be deceitful. But it also felt important to know what was being said on the other side of the door. At once, I heard my name.

"Sybil learned to ride a horse. She's patrolling for me already."

"With Johnny," Mama cut in. "Are you going to ask Johnny to help lead your spy ring, too?"

"No, General Washington said to tell no one outside of our family. That's the point of a secret, Abigail."

He meant it to lighten the mood. I doubted it worked. Mama was a lioness, saying, "And did you tell His Excellency that your only children old enough to help are daughters?"

"He didn't ask. He only assumed with all my other responsibilities as a colonel and with the Sons of Liberty that my oldest children would assist me. Besides, I think the girls are capable. Just as capable as boys."

"But it's not how girls are supposed to act," Mama insisted. I counted three beats of silence, then Mama said, "What if someone catches wind of what we're doing and blabs? Let us not forget Nathan Hale. Do you want that for your daughters? Or for any of us?"

"Of course not. And you know as well as I that Hale was ill prepared."

Everyone school-aged and above knew that name. He'd been a spy for General Washington only last year, a schoolteacher. Mr. Hale had believed his profession, an honorable one, would've put him above suspicion. But, no. He'd gone beyond enemy lines and had been caught within a week. Alas, he'd been hung within a week. Mr. Hale had become infamous, not for anything he'd unearthed as a spy, but for his final words. *I only regret that I have but one life to lose for my country.*

Those words had breathed an extra dose of patriotism into Papa's already patriotic body.

Papa went on, "He crossed into enemy lines as himself, with no cover story beyond wanting to teach. And we … we'll be prepared. We'll do no crossing. Others will do the crossing for us. I'm known as a farmer. If I were to go into the City of New York, it'd raise suspicion. So, we'll coordinate the sending of others who have business being there."

"I don't like it," Mama said. "What protections will our family have?"

"Codes," Papa said.

"Codes," Mama repeated, and if I knew my mama, her eyes rolled, as if Papa was explaining the rules of some game.

"Yes. It's fanciful, really."

"Fanciful?" Mama sighed. "This is serious, Henry."

"Of course it is—and everything serious we do will be done in codes or secret writing or hidden messages. It's designed to only be discovered by those we wish to discover it."

Mama said, "I don't know."

Papa said, "I do. I don't wish to put us in greater danger, but spies will end this war more quickly. Isn't that want you want?"

"I want peace."

"And peace you'll have," Papa told her, "along with freedom. But I need the girls to help me pull this off."

Papa needed me, but he also needed Rebecca, who was sleeping instead of skulking around the house and tiring herself out. At that, I noiselessly returned upstairs. In the morning, we'd begin ... we'd begin codes, secret writing, and hidden messages, too.

# CHAPTER 12

"Close your eyes," Papa said to Rebecca and me.

There was no telling who listened first. In an instant, behind my eyelids I only saw black with a hint of red from the morning's sun. If only its glow also brought warmth, but Mama was preparing the hearth to help with that.

"Now," Papa said. "Write what I say."

He had already outfitted Rebecca and me with quill pens, wet with ink.

With my left hand, I found and secured my paper that was laid out before us on Mama's worktable in the kitchen.

Papa recited, "I solemnly swear I'll be the best spy the colonists have ever seen."

I smiled.

Ink to my paper, I began writing, ignoring the squeals and cries and general loudness of my other siblings in the various rooms of our first floor. I didn't dare peek at my paper. Papa's voice may've cracked with humor as he gave us our sentence to write, but I did want to be the best dang spy, and certainly the better of the two spies-in-training performing this task.

I heard, "Open your eyes."

I tilted my head, to better read my words. They slanted upward, like a table with legs shorter on one side. Then, where

I had lifted my quill to begin a new word, the letters jumped slightly up or down. Where I'd begun a new line, some of the wording overlapped.

However, I noticed, as I peeked at Rebecca's paper, with similar highs and lows to her sentence, I had spelled all my words correctly. She left out the *n* in solemnly. Rebecca laid her pen across the word and raised her eyes to Papa's. "What's next?"

"Do it again. And again. Practice to keep your lettering straight. I'll be back soon, with a surprise."

With an eager dip in my ink, I set to work. I was at the *n* of solemnly when I heard Papa say, "Eyes closed, Rebecca."

I smiled once more.

Papa returned, what seemed like hours later. My hand ached from writing. Funny how holding a quill used different muscles than while grasping a hoe or wringing clothes or controlling reins.

Speaking of the latter, I leaned to my side to better see out the front window. There was Star, looking back at me. Why was I surprised? His pastures stretched along and around our home, which allowed me to see him from most anywhere in the house. It was comforting, especially when I knew he so often kept an eye on me, as if saying, *I see you in there. Now, when are you coming out here to be with me?*

It wouldn't be long now until our usual midday training, unless Papa had more work for me, which seemed likely. He currently readied a few vials on the tabletop. A few vials of what, I wasn't sure. Rebecca's hands twitched in her lap, as if she wanted to reach out and grab one to examine. I fought the same urge. "Is it tea?" I asked.

Papa shook his head. "Put these on."

He laid down gloves.

Rebecca and I exchanged glances. On this matter, we both shared the question of … why do we need those? These weren't the elbow-length gloves that the older society women wore. They were work gloves, which were only ever used for outdoor chores. Chores that otherwise caused blisters or calluses.

Dutifully, we began to reach for the gloves, just as Mama entered the room with two squirming chickens in her arms. "Gloves, how perfect for the yard and barn work. Out you go."

"Abigail," Papa said. "I was about to show the girls—"

"I'm about to ready these chickens for our evening meal." She passed one of the wriggling chickens to Papa. "I need the table from the girls. They've been in here all morning, instead of out doing their chores."

Being caught between two parents is no place any child ever wants to be. Finally, Papa relented. "Girls, out you go. When you're done, come straight to me. We'll continue with the surprise."

Papa took the small vials and put them back into his pockets with a wink. My sister and I swiped the gloves then skedaddled. Our well-worn boots stood at attention by the door and we slipped into them with ease. As we left, bundled against the cold, the sound of Mama's butcher knife slicing neck and hitting the tabletop chased us outside.

Rebecca and I tackled the hen house together. We mucked and brought in fresh hay. Rebecca collected the eggs, fewer in the wintertime, and I banged a shovel into the trough to break up the ice that had gathered. We worked quickly, not having to keep an eye out for snakes or hornets. The coldness blissfully removed those threats, along with ticks and poison ivy. It was one of the few blessings of wintertime farming.

We moved through the rest of our chores, and I had to admit, having Rebecca home, instead of at school, wasn't half bad. It also wasn't full good, especially when I took a step toward Star, but heard Rebecca say, "Enjoy your time with Star. I'm going to see to Papa's surprise."

I stopped in my tracks, though my heart kept going toward my boy.

"I'll be right in," I said to my sister, then my feet chased after my heart. At the fence line, I removed my glove to rub Star's head, my hand brushing over his white marking. He lowered his head, asking for more. "Sorry, boy. But I'll be back as soon as I can."

He didn't doubt me, he wouldn't, but I felt him watching me all the way back inside. When I entered the house, I heard Papa's voice. "Sybil, is your sister on her way?" Then an, "Oh, Rebecca, I thought you were Sybil. My mistake."

I quickened my pace toward the kitchen. Papa was setting up the vials again on the table. He was very careful, as if afraid they'd spill and stain Mama's tabletop. Papa wasn't a mutton-head. But I currently doubted his eyesight for confusing his children.

Mama sometimes mixed up our names. But considering she once called me "Mary-Abigail-Rebecca-Samantha"—the last one being the name of our hound—I figured her mistake had been because of pure exhaustion.

However, Papa … I'd like to hear his excuse. I frowned. Rebecca and I *did* look alike. Both tall. Both freckled. Both brown hair. Both our hairs plaited into a single braid, too. Papa wouldn't remember from earlier than I was wearing blue and Rebecca purple.

I joined them at the table, standing on Papa's right side. It put him between my sister and me. "Ah, there you are," he said to me, then looked between Rebecca and me. "I wonder." In a breath, Rebecca and I were back to back. "Would you look at that," he said, taking measure of us so close together. "Rebecca has taken you in height, Sybil."

Rebecca twisted to face me. She smiled so big her face may as well have been simply a smile.

*Would you look at that*, I thought—bitterly—in my head. Out loud, I redirected our focus back to the table: "What do we have here, Papa?"

"What we have here," Papa began, "is modern-day magic."

I tilted my head toward the tea-colored vials. Papa handed my sister and me quills and blank paper.

"Dip your quills in. Watchfully," he added. "Then I want you to write something on your paper. Anything. A secret, even. Yes, a secret."

I thought on it. What I had to say wasn't hush-hush, exactly.

My secret was merely a private thought—which anyone could likely guess. I began to write *I'm glad Star is mine and only mine* but as I touched my quill to the paper and dragged the instrument down to craft the first letter, nothing happened.

The paper remained blank.

"Papa?" I said. "My ink isn't working."

"Oh yes, it is," he said. "The ink is invisible."

Invisible. How sly. How inventive. "But how?"

Papa smiled. "Science. The right mixture of this and that. Others know the details better than I. What's important is that I know how to use it. Go on, finish writing, girls."

I did, the sensation of not knowing what I was writing similar to having my eyes closed earlier, but easier, since I could watch how my hand glided across the empty page.

Rebecca took longer to finish. To be fair, she was later to begin, her lip tucked between her teeth as she thought about what secret to write.

Papa rubbed his hands together. "Now, let's reveal what you've written."

Before we could react, my sister's and my hands were empty and Papa held one of the papers—I couldn't be sure whose— over Mama's candlesticks.

Once, I believed my beloved swivel chair to be my favorite hocus-pocus, but this—here—the revealing of nothing to something—was double … no, triple the abracadabra of Mr. Jefferson's invention. I held my breath, watching as the fire's heat interacted with the mysterious chemical solution, the words emerging. Forming.

"Sybil," Papa said, having the clearest view of the paper. "Come now, we all know this."

Beside me, Rebecca stiffened. Was it to what I had written? Had I wounded her by saying I was glad to have Star all to myself, when I knew she wanted a horse of her own, too? Then, as Rebecca did something so bold as to snatch her paper— the one not yet revealed—from Papa's grasp, I realized, no, Rebecca's sudden reaction was because she didn't want her secret revealed.

What had she written?

# CHAPTER 13

The question lingered in my mind, but—my goodness—I was too busy swiveling between Sybil the Spy and Sybil the Farmer and Sybil the Daughter and Sybil the Older Sister and Sybil the Horse Trainer to dwell too much on what Rebecca had secretly written.

Besides, at the moment, Johnny Whitaker and I were doing one of our loops and I was currently dwelling on how I couldn't tell him about my Sybil the Spy efforts, a role I found myself thinking of as soon as my eyes blinked open with the gurgle of our rooster, the poor thing sounding as if he had something lodged in his throat. Mama assured us he was fine—or else he would've been on our plates long ago.

Still, I held little faith in the rooster's permanence on our farm, so I refused to call him Rodger like the rest of the family. Once, I'd named our pig. A mistake. That pig had joined us for supper for the holidays.

But that blessed pig and rooster just distracted me for a moment from whisper-yelling at Johnny Whitaker: *Papa's a spy-ring leader! I'm helping! I'm a spy! Just like Mr. Paul Revere!*

It helped to bite my teeth together really hard.

"Sybil?"

"Mmhmm," I said without opening my mouth. I could only imagine his reaction if I told him what I've been up to. He'd fall off his horse.

"Everything all right?"

I nodded.

Johnny Whitaker's eyebrows furrowed. "If you say so. Want to turn around at the creek?"

"I should get back now, actually."

That really shocked him. I never wanted to end our rides early. But, Papa likely had the mail by now. And, all at once, it seemed like each new day brought a new spy-related letter.

At first, the letters were innocent-looking enough. And were filled with innocent farming questions for Papa. But when Papa held the paper over a flame, that all changed. The invisible ink showed itself in the spaces between each line of the letter.

It became two letters in one, with one letter innocent and the other incriminating.

It was why we burned the letters as soon as we were done with them.

In the first few incriminating letters, the messages were instructional for Papa, providing guidance and expectations for his spy ring. The goal of it was to gather information about the British activities. Their day-to-day operations. What types of supplies they had. What types they didn't. General Washington wished to know where the British troops were, where they were going next, and how dangerous they'd be once they got wherever they were going.

What we were doing could really make a difference in this war.

It filled me with pride. And I badly wanted to rave about it to my friend.

Back at my house, Johnny Whitaker and I parted ways and I rushed inside.

"Good," Papa said at once. "You're home early. Rebecca!"

Rebecca came running.

"This letter's different," Papa said, tapping it. "Our work's beginning. Our real work."

My insides danced like they were filled with fireflies and butterflies and anything with wings.

Papa went on, "This letter contains the making of codes. See here"—Papa pointed—"one number. One word. Write them down, Rebecca."

She all but leapt to grab the leather-bound book on the table.

"Once that book is full and we have all the code combinations, the next letters we receive will only contain numbers. We'll use our book to decode the messages."

Over the next few days, we held each letter over the flames to reveal the combinations of numbers and words.

Hill was 469

Attack was 38

Boston was 733

Horse was 472

Damage was 125

Artillery was 46

General Washington was 711

Soon, we had hundreds and hundreds and hundreds of codes.

We'd fallen into a routine. Rebecca read from the letters. I recorded. My penmanship was better. Papa said our process was flawless. Superb. He praised his undercover daughters for working so well together and grinned extra big when Rebecca read the name and number assigned to him. I proudly wrote it into our book.

While our codebook was filling, Papa was called away again with his regiment. At first, Rebecca and I were nervous about not having Papa there to double check our work, but we truly did work well together.

And before we knew it, our book was filled. That was when the clandestine letters changed, just as Papa said they would. They were no longer guidance about how Papa should run his spy ring. They no longer contained a word plus a number to fill our book. Now, in today's letter, it was the first time the invisible ink revealed only numbers.

It was time to use our codebook to decode the message.

It felt like Christmas morning.

"Think we should wait until Papa returns?" Rebecca asked.

I licked my lips, excited to decode the numbers. "It won't do any harm to have the message ready for him, right?

Rebecca smiled. "615 is the first."

The number hung in the air—an exhilarating mystery—and Papa not being here was forgotten. I flipped through the pages, licking my lips again, readying myself to speak. Finally, I'd found it, one of the later entries, and read from our codebook, "Messenger."

"657."

I trailed my finger lower until: "Visit."

My sister and I locked eyes. Papa had mentioned that we'd house his spies. Had the time come?

"19th," she said, a question in her voice. "Not 19, but with the *th*."

"Go on, then," I said, impatient to decode another number. "215."

I moved to the earlier pages. "February."

My pulse quickened. February 19th was within the week.

Like a game of tag, Rebecca read and I responded, reading and searching as quickly as humanly possible.

499, 593, 465, 109.

*If safe hang clothier.*

# CHAPTER 14

A messenger was to visit the nineteen of February. If safe, hang clothier.

Our very first coded message. My toes wiggled under my sheets or in my slippers or in my work boots or while dangling from Star—depending on what I was doing while the words ran through my head.

If I thought it was difficult not to tell Johnny Whitaker before that I was helping General Washington spy, it was even harder now.

"Could I tell him?" I even asked Papa before he'd even had his boots off after returning home. "More than ever, we need to make sure the property is safe. If he knew, Johnny Whitaker could keep a keener eye."

"I'd hope Johnny's eyes are keen enough as it is." Papa tugged off a boot. "But, you are right in saying we need to make sure the property is safe. You still train Star midday, correct?"

"Correct, sir."

"If you can bear the cold, could you do another loop then?"

"By myself?"

I could've caught flies with how my mouth fell open. I was

shocked Papa would let me do it alone. Shocked but very glad for this small freedom.

"I think you're ready. Unless you think otherwise?"

"I'm ready."

Papa removed his other boot. "Splendid."

"But Mama …" I began, nervous about her reaction.

Papa frowned. "I'll speak with your mama."

I almost wished him good luck.

I liked my nightly rides with Johnny Whitaker. It was nice to have someone to talk to, even if I had to be careful what we spoke about. But it truly was splendid being out on Star just the two of us during my new afternoon patrol. The biggest danger I came across in the dead of winter was the risk of the tip of my nose freezing over then falling off.

Some days I didn't ride Star, only walked beside him on the frozen, snow-packed ground. I was worried his poor hooves would bruise or that he'd slip. As it was, his tail swished.

Tail swishing served a few different purposes:

To get the flies off—except the winter had done away with those insects.

When the saddle was a nuisance—but today we didn't have one on.

To let me know he was in pain—only he wasn't limping.

When he was concentrating hard on each footfall—which could be the case.

Or, my boy could've been simply content—and swished his tail like our hound Samantha wagged hers.

"Are you happy, boy?" I asked Star.

He showed me his teeth.

I showed him mine back, though mine chattered. But at least it was only from the cold and not out of fear. We never saw anyone during our rides or walks.

And, on the morning of February nineteenth, Papa declared it was safe for our very first messenger to arrive.

Hurrah!

I'd never been more excited to launder our clothing. It was likely the first time I had ever had such a thought. I usually loathed the process of washing our clothes.

It began with urine, human urine, mostly my brothers', who were eager to help in this portion of the laundry. The idea of soaking our clothier in it—in pee—always had my nose scrunching. But Mama insisted it was the best way to get out stains. So, urine it was.

The fabrics soaked, then on the morning of our laundering we'd begin cleaning. Water was hauled. Water was heated. Then one-by-one, we'd scrub each article with our homemade soap, using rocks and a washboard to help remove the dirt and grime. From there, excess water was wrung out, my hands aching by the end. Finally, everything was hung on the line, the breeze having the easiest job of us all.

It was an all-day event. It was also something we didn't do often since it was such a chore. And it was why—ever since we received the message to hang clothier—Mama grumbled about doing extra wash when we'd only done it two weeks earlier. In the winter months, we laundered even less, and if not for the message, our dirty sheets and shirts and pants and under-things would've kept piling up for another month, maybe longer.

The upside to having done our laundry not long ago was how quickly our pile vanished this morning. My hands only half-ached as I propped a basket of wet clothing on my hip and tottered toward the line, strung high between two trees. When I was younger, I climbed up and down from a step stool to reach the rope. Now I could reach, even though I had to roll onto my tiptoes.

Rebecca was already at the drying line with her own basket, two shirts dangling. In the summer months, the sun was ravenous and sucked all the water from our clothing within hours. But in the wintertime, it was as if the sun wasn't as hungry and the process of evaporation took hours and hours and hours and sometimes days.

But today, it could take as long as it wanted. Our signal was the hanging of clothes—and not the taking down of clothes.

"I've already begun and you'll only be in my way."

Rebecca barked the words without even turning to face me. She reached up and pinned pants to the line—without, I noticed, having to roll onto her tiptoes. I'd often prided myself on being tall for my age, the only one of my siblings standing taller than even Mama. Now Rebecca had eclipsed me. It was as if her long arms and gangly legs snickered at the fact I was one year, nine months, and nineteen days older.

A snowflake landed on my nose. I brushed it away and replied, "We each have a basket. We might as well each hang."

"I hang faster." She didn't comment on her gangly or longly limbs, but I knew she was thinking how she reached the line better than me. I knew she recalled the moment in the kitchen with Papa when he'd placed us back to back, her head higher. "And, I'm quite capable of signaling to our messenger on my own."

"You'd like that," I said with an edge to my voice.

"I would." Rebecca faced me, but also looked beyond me, toward the house, toward where Papa stood at the window, surveying all that was going on. I bet his eyes fell on the line, watching as the signal came to life, but I also saw him looking down the long drive, peering deep into the bare woods, scrutinizing the lands on the far side of our creek, whitening with snow each minute that passed.

"Fine," I said to my sister. "I'll go for a ride."

Star didn't object. Nor did I object to the idea of spotting the messenger first, then hotfooting it back to signal—loud and clear—to Papa that our messenger was on his way.

Star and I moved slowly, not wanting to startle our messenger, and the sounds of winter were eerily quiet. No birds chirping, no leaves rustling in the trees, the creek soundlessly, barely trickling. But that left room for the sound of a snapped twig, caused either by our messenger or an animal, one that didn't hibernate. A deer? A weasel? A raccoon?

A cough came next, along with a silly image of a coughing raccoon—that politely pulled out a handkerchief to cover his mouth. I smiled to myself and said, "Whoa," to Star. He slowed then stopped, without a tug on the reins. His breath escaped from his nostrils, forming a small cloud in front of him, and I absently stroked Star's neck while searching through the trees, until—a-ha—I spotted the coughing man. He didn't prowl through the forest, as I had for some reason expected him to do as a spy. But the man sauntered beyond the trees, straight up our drive, leaving his footsteps behind. He began to whistle, as if signaling to us *Here I come!*

"Ho," I prodded Star.

And my boy went, straight to Papa.

I wanted Papa to hear from me—and not from the whistle—that our messenger was approaching. Our whole family waited in the parlor. Mama sat stiffly in a chair. Little Abigail, almost a year old, toddled around the room, hands out, feet shuffling. She'd fall. She'd stand again. But she was determined to chase the other five. Rebecca made six, standing next to me. I stood next to Papa. I felt like a lowland between the two.

Then, the man appeared, his hat first, coming over the hill of our drive. He bobbed. Bounced, in a way.

His hat was black, speckled with snow. Up and down his hat went, until his face joined the motion.

That was enough of him for Mama. She ushered my siblings out of the room, trying to take me with them.

"Sybil and Rebecca can stay," Papa said.

"Very well," Mama said, but in a tone where you knew it wasn't "very well" for even a second.

Happy to stay, I turned back to the window. The man was

young. Younger than I had thought him to be. Mr. Paul Revere was older than Papa. But this man was somewhere between my age and Papa's.

Once he overcame the hill, I saw that our messenger held a bag. He was dressed smartly, from his heavy jacket all the way to his somehow shiny black shoes that seemed to reflect the snow.

With a smile, he glanced at our hanging clothier.

I smiled, too. I couldn't wait for him to get inside. I couldn't wait to learn why he was sent to us. I couldn't wait to hear what this man had to say.

# CHAPTER 15

Initially, the man didn't say much. Not even his name.

His right eye was bruised.

Once inside, I realized that bounce of his was actually a limp.

My brothers and sisters sounded like a herd of elephants above us. The man glanced up, smiling. He glanced at Rebecca and me. "Sounds like you have quite the family."

"Big," Papa said, returning his smile. "I'm Colonel Ludington."

The man nodded. I guessed he already knew that. Then offered, "I'm Enoch Crosby."

I'd never met someone named Enoch before. Standing tall next to Papa, I was already intrigued.

Papa led him to a chair by the fire. Mr. Crosby rubbed his hands together, stopping every few seconds to hold his palms out to the heat. I mouthed to Papa, *drink?* and Papa jerked his head, as if he should've thought of that. "Where are my manners? Rebecca," he said, "can you bring some tea?"

While I usually liked to be the one Papa turned to, I didn't mind staying in the room with this mysterious man. I took a seat across from him on the couch, hands in my lap, as Rebecca all but sprinted from the room.

Not that there was a real need for her to hurry. She wasn't missing anything. At first, Papa didn't say any more, as if knowing this man needed a few moments to gather himself. Eventually Papa asked him from where he traveled.

"Fishkill."

It wasn't far, one of the closer towns. With a four-beat walk, I imagined Star and I would've been able to get there in three hours. With a two-beat trot, in well under two. Not that Papa had ever let Star and me leave the property alone. Walking on foot, I assumed, would take longer. Perhaps five hours. Maybe more, with his limp. I was curious about that limp.

Papa said, "Makes sense they sent you here."

"I'm obliged to be here. Warmer, I'd say. I usually hide out in caves or hollows. Certainly can't go home." He gave an artificial-sounding laugh, then quickly added, "I won't be needing to stay long. Just a day or two to get my wits about me."

"Had a rough go of it, did you?"

The man licked his lips. "Some. I was pretending to be a Loyalist, part of a group of them. Well, we got captured. I've got this," Mr. Crosby said, and pulled a paper from his breast pocket. Papa took it, read it. Without thinking, he passed it to me. That surely swelled my chest with pride.

"You always keep it hidden there?" Papa asked, while I read.

"Usually my boot."

"We'll find someplace better."

"Fine by me," Mr. Crosby said

The paper explained how Mr. Crosby was actually a Patriot, under orders to infiltrate the Loyalists and British. If caught, our side was to do a mock trial and release him.

It was exactly what had happened. But before Mr. Crosby could discreetly show the document to his capturers, he and the Loyalist group were roughly arrested. He had the bruise and twisted ankle to prove it.

He said, "I've information to pass on. In Fishkill, they said to wait until I arrived here so it can be encrypted."

"Sybil—and Rebecca," Papa said, as my sister reentered the room with a tray, "can help with the coding."

If he had any unhappiness with two young girls being tasked with such an important job, Mr. Crosby didn't show it. He only sipped from his mug, letting the steam wash over his stubble-covered face.

I liked him immediately for it.

And, over the course of the next day, I liked him more and more. He was funny, even. "Why is England the wettest country?" he asked. Then answered, "Because Kings and Queens have been reigning there for nearly a thousand years."

In between our laughter, we coded his message, me looking up the words and Rebecca using the invisible ink to write out the corresponding letters. In the end, we communicated the whereabouts and the number of Loyalists Mr. Crosby had seen in the surrounding areas. Off the secret letter would go to General Washington with our next mailings. The fact the postal office was on our lands made the task an easy one for Star and me.

"I'll go up to Manhattan next," he said. That morning, it was just Mr. Crosby and I in the sewing room. He'd told me the room reminded him fondly of a shoemaker's shop where he'd once apprenticed.

*Manhattan, as in the British's headquarters*, I thought to myself. But I also thought how it was a city, where women could be more than farmers. At the moment, though, it was a dangerous place to be for any Patriot, surrounded by the enemy. "How'd you become a spy, Mr. Crosby?"

"I was asked to be one."

"Me, too."

He smiled. "What your family is doing isn't a small thing, you know."

"Mama's made that clear." It was a bold thing for me to say, but if there was a man who seemed akin to boldness, Mr. Crosby was that man. He was quiet when he first arrived, but he'd since found his voice and was more than willing to use it.

He said, "You're lucky to have your mama."

I looked up from my sewing. Those words sounded different, sadder. I quickly changed the subject. "So you're a shoemaker? You do have very nice shoes."

"I should. Worked in that apprenticeship for seven years, before I opened my own shop. When the war began, I enlisted. Wish I could've done more back then, but I fell ill and was sent home. I guess being in the army put some ants in my pants, though, because I couldn't seem to sit still."

I smiled at his use of *ants in my pants*. It was something

I would say. I probably had said it recently.

"I decided to go from town to town making shoes," he went on. "That's when I ran into a Loyalist, who thought me to be one, too. After that, I had a mind to join up with the Continental Army again. I tried, but they didn't want me to be a soldier."

I finished, "They asked you to be a spy."

"That's right."

What a history he had. He'd been all over. He'd seen so much. It felt as if this man could've been anything, done anything. At the moment, I liked the kinship of us both being spies.

Mr. Crosby went on, "I'm a pretend Loyalist now. Only a few folks know the truth, yourself included." A smile grew on my face, though it faded quickly as his voice took on that sad tone again. "My parents, my brother, my little sisters ... I haven't seen them in ages. They all think I'm a Loyalist."

"And they're all Patriots?"

His head bobbed, while his chest filled with air. "They're Patriots."

The poor man, so smart-looking in his suit, had such a long face. And I realized, even with all his worldliness, he still had something that held him back: The secret he kept from his family. A secret that put a great divide between them.

I didn't want to pry with more questions, but I found myself watching him. All that watching led to an idea. "That documentation you have, the one that says you're actually a Patriot ... I've a thought to where you can hide it."

"Do you, Miss Sybil?" Some of his lightheartedness returned to his voice.

It took me a while to get it all done, but when I had completed folding and sewing and stitching, the tiny slip of paper was concealed within one of the cloth buttons that ran down his vest.

"And now, if you ever find yourself in trouble," I said. "You can easily rip off the button and hand it over."

"Well aren't you clever. You sure know how to take care of your guests."

I was the only person in the room to hear his words. No Papa. No Mama. No Rebecca. But they felt great to hear, just the same. I most certainly liked Mr. Crosby being around. If only he didn't have to leave.

# CHAPTER 16

The time came too quickly for Mr. Crosby to take his spy skills to the City of New York.

"But you'll return?" I asked him. We were in the sewing room once again. This time, Rebecca was with us. She even had claimed the swivel chair.

"Oh yes," Mr. Crosby said. "I'll be back within the month once my mind is dripping with clandestine information."

Mama entered the room at that exact moment. "Is that so? I've no need to hang clothier again so soon. Certainly not with all this snow we're getting."

A silence filled the room, a rather awkward one. Rebecca broke it. "What if we signaled in a different way?"

"How?" I asked.

"Well," Rebecca said, beginning slowly, until a smile quickened on her face. "Remember Mr. Paul Revere? Lanterns were hung as a signal. We can hang two each evening, when safe. But if there are any signs of danger for Mr. Crosby, we'll light only one."

"Splendid," Mr. Crosby said. "And I'll whistle, like before."

I twisted my lips. The idea *was* a good one, but it stung like a hornet in the hen house had gotten me. I so often felt a connection with Mr. Paul Revere as I galloped on Star's back. An idea inspired by him should've come from my brain and my lips, and not my sister's.

But with Mr. Crosby leaving, there was little time to wallow. On foot, the journey would've been a cold one and taken Mr. Crosby a full day of nonstop marching from our part of New York to Manhattan. But, while we were outside saying our good-byes, Papa gave Mr. Crosby extra money to buy a horse over in the town of Pawling. His sore ankle would thank him. That walk would still be mighty cold, but at least it'd take little more than an hour.

"I'll name her Moon," he told me, giving Star a good rubbing on his flank. "To go with your Star. When I return, we'll go for a ride together. How does that sound?"

I beamed. Star did, too. Horses could smile, just as a person could. All teeth and sometimes lots of gums.

Johnny Whitaker came as Mr. Crosby left.

I already had Star saddled.

"Who was that?"

"Oh, that's Mr. Crosby."

Papa said if anyone asked about our spy to be honest about his name. And also about who Mr. Crosby was prior to joining our spy ring, minus the spying parts. "When bending the truth," Papa had said, "It's always best to stick as close to the facts as possible. Or else you'll forget what facts you first said if you're asked again." So I said, "He's a shoemaker, goes house to house selling them."

"Your boots don't look new," Johnny Whitaker remarked.

"It's not as if I'd wear my new ones in all this muck. Really, Johnny Whitaker."

He laughed.

Then I asked, "What do you think about being a shoemaker?"

"I prefer blacksmithing."

"Yes," I began, but then I stopped from adding: *But how about for me?* Johnny Whitaker would only make fun of me for thinking something through I couldn't do.

∾

At least I could be a girl who spied. *Sybil the Spy.* That would never grow old.

After Mr. Crosby left, Papa recruited a few trusted men from his militia. The thing was, once farming season began in two months, Papa's encampment would all return home. They'd be needed on their lands. For now, they were Papa's. The men scouted for him, then they reported to our home with any information they unearthed.

They unearthed a lot.

Our new spies came and went from our home almost nightly, guided by nothing but the moon reflecting off the fresh snow. Their signal came in the form of a warble, as if a bird, whistling *Here we come!*

The first man was slow to approach our house, even with

our two lanterns being lit. And, I knew why.

Mama.

As the timeline went, Papa had become colonel last year. His encampment had been quickly built on our lands. But from the start, Mama had felt like the camp was too close to our home. It wasn't as if she could see the men, hear them, or even smell them. But she knew they were there.

And they were bashful about seeing her because she'd proven she was a tough cookie. She'd made that clear at a May Day festival, where a bunch of the men, who'd later join Papa's regiment, were arm wrestling.

They wheedled Papa to have a seat, to put his elbow on the table, and show them his stuff. He refused, not because he was a coward. I'd seen Papa bend an arm before. Really fast, too. But Papa had sliced his hand on a rock out in the fields the day before. Squeezing another man's hand wouldn't have felt good.

Mama knew it. She also knew Papa wouldn't like losing. He'd been about to give in to their taunts, but then Mama had stepped in. She handed Papa one of my siblings she'd been holding—probably Derick—and she sat down. A man versus a woman, it was a first for us. Everyone's eyes were as big as supper plates. Her opponent was slow to take her hand, but she nodded for him to do so.

The match had been quick, quicker than anyone would've guessed. But I wasn't surprised. By that point, Mama had been carrying around heavy babies and toddlers for a decade. And when she didn't have a kid in her arms, she was hauling wood or helping with the plow or stirring something thick on the stove. Mama was as brawny as a man, brawnier, in fact, than the man across from her. He didn't have a lot of meat on his bones, but Mama had a healthy amount, no doubt keeping a few pounds with every brother or sister she added to our family.

Right after she'd won, Mama smiled sweetly and motioned for someone else to sit down across from her, even though I thought she'd only been feigning that she wanted to keep going. Truth be told, I'd been surprised she sat down at all. If it were me I had no doubt she'd scold me saying, "Sybil, arm wrestling isn't proper for a lady."

But Mama did it for Papa. Just that once. Nobody else had the mettle to challenge her and risk being beaten by Mrs. Henry Ludington.

That day Mama's reputation as a woman not to be messed with was set in stone. But now a few of those men were coming to our door. Even though Mama wasn't happy about it, she still led them to the fire and offered them a hot meal. She helped to darn their clothing and always sent them on their way with extra bread.

I'd never heard so many thank yous.

She often said to Papa, "What is this? I feel as if I'm running an inn."

She said it with indignation; annoyed these men were in her home. But I didn't mind bringing them food, making sure they had what they needed, or hauling in extra wood. And as much as I hated sewing, I even enjoyed mending their things, as they told me tales. Running an inn sounded fun, to me, at least.

Mama always followed their exit with a big exhale. It was clear what it meant: Relief they were gone. Relief that planting season began soon and—soon—all the men would return to their own homes to tend to their own business.

For now, they came.

I coded.

I mailed the intelligence to General Washington.

I patrolled on Star.

Each time I returned from my nightly ride with Johnny Whitaker, I'd close the chicken coop, and then I'd run inside to the warmth. And each time, I had nearly the same exchange with Mama and Papa.

First, Papa: "Did you see anything peculiar?"

Me: "No."

Then Mama always said: "Good. Thank goodness that Johnny's with you, in case you ever stumble upon more of those Loyalists."

"There's no one out there besides Papa's troops," I always said.

Never fail, she balked at that—at the troops. Sometimes she called them scarecrows, meaning their only purpose was scaring things off, which she couldn't be entirely unhappy about, right?

But she forever ended with: "I don't see the need for you

roaming about on that horse of yours. I'd rather you stay home."

Of course she did. If Mama had her way, I'd never leave the farm, until I had a husband to bring me to *his* farm.

That night during supper, I heard a warble. Rebecca and I locked eyes. A spy was on his way. We'd have work to do soon. We coded almost daily, with whatever information the warblers had to say. Papa stood from the dining table and crossed the room to brush aside Mama's curtains and cup his hands against the window to see out.

"Well, I'll be," Papa said.

# CHAPTER 17

Mr. Crosby was back! And, the warmer weather followed him in. That night, snow changed to rain, big old raindrops the size of marbles. By morning, the icicles that dangled from our porch began to melt, dripping on a barn cat as she passed underneath. It startled her, sending her darting for cover and my little brothers chasing after. Soon, the many inches of snow were speckled with fat rain holes that combined together, creating hollows that revealed the long-forgotten greens and browns of the ground.

Beneath that ground, were my fireflies.

I couldn't wait for them to emerge in a few weeks.

When I turned out Star in his pasture, he went as mad as a March hare; fitting, as it was now late March. We let his excitement wind down, but his hoofs started stomping again, his tail swishing, too, when Mr. Crosby brought Moon toward his fence.

Papa said the best way for two horses to meet was turning them out together in the pasture. Star was easygoing, my happy-go-lucky boy. And he happily chased after Moon, but in a way that didn't make Moon scared. No biting, no kicking. They were fast friends.

"Cut from the same cloth," Mr. Crosby said. "But I could use some help training her."

It was music to my ears. But before I could be Sybil the Horse Trainer, we had coding to do. Rebecca waited for us at the table, my book of codes beside her. I felt a pang of guilt, with how she looked at Mr. Crosby and me, knowing we both had been tending to our horses.

Perhaps Mr. Crosby knew, too. "Rebecca," he said. "I was just talking to Sybil about training Moon. I could sure use your help, too."

She straightened in her chair, a grin appearing on her freckled face.

That Mr. Crosby was a good man. I'd said it before. I'd say it again.

I enjoyed his riddles, too, and during the month he'd been away, I'd thought of one for him.

While he worked on writing down his message for General Washington, I asked, "Why can't a nose be twelve inches long?"

His quill paused midair.

Rebecca twisted her lips. I didn't think she knew the answer. But did Mr. Crosby?

His eyes narrowed. He thought about it long and hard. Then, he shook his head, a smile already on his face about hearing the answer.

I blurted out, "Because then it'd be a foot!"

A laugh rumbled up Mr. Crosby's throat and he dropped his forehead into his hand, leaving behind a smear of ink.

Rebecca giggled, glancing toward the kitchen in case we were being too loud for Mama. But Mama didn't appear, and

Mr. Crosby said, "I've another one for you girls. What do you call a doe with no eyes?" He waited, one, two, three seconds.

I said, "I have no idea."

He chuckled to himself. I still didn't get it. But then Rebecca's face lit up and she started laughing. She said, "No eye-deer. As in … no idea!"

Mr. Crosby pointed at her in a "you win" type of way. Her face brightened even more. I was happy when Papa walked in, a letter in his hand from a courier.

We broke the wax seal.

As always, the letter appeared to be any old note.

"Will you do the honors?" Papa asked Mr. Crosby.

Our spy held the letter up to a candle.

The heat revealed the hidden ink.

Mr. Crosby read the first number.

I looked it up in my book, reciting the associated word.

Rebecca wrote it down.

Around and around we went as Papa watched on.

I made a game of it, flipping the pages of my codebook as quickly as possible, spouting off words.

*Wanted by Howe* ….

As in the British General Howe. My heart rate quickened. It only made me move faster.

*Dead or alive* ….

*Bounty of three hundred guineas* ….

*For* ….

Rebecca said, "602."

My eyes jumped down the page, having a hard time focusing out of fear. *All even numbers*, I told myself, in the hope the detail would be a calming distraction. But then I saw the name, and any calmness went straight out the window. I didn't waste another breath to say it.

*Enoch Crosby.*

# CHAPTER 18

Mr. Crosby was a wanted man.

It tore at my heart.

Papa insisted Mr. Crosby should stay. And that we'd protect him.

Mr. Crosby insisted he should leave.

Mama stood by, her arms crossed. We all knew what she'd insist.

In the end, Mama won, without saying a single word.

It was a rare sun-filled day when Mr. Crosby headed toward Moon with a saddle and his shoe kit slung over his shoulder. We'd never gotten to train or to ride, but I knew his safety was more important than both those things. And I knew him staying here, where the Loyalists already had their sights set on Papa, could be dangerous. It didn't make me drag my feet any less, though.

I asked him, "You won't be back this time, will you?"

"Never say never, but it's not likely if it'll bring danger to your family. Family's important, Sybil, and"—Mr. Crosby paused—"family shouldn't be taken for granted."

I remembered how his family wrongly believed him to be a Loyalist. "How long has it been since you've seen yours?"

"Since I became a spy. My two sisters remind me a lot of

you and Rebecca, in fact. It's been nice to be around you two. Can I ask something of you, Sybil?"

"Anything."

He was slow to start again. "If I'm caught, will you help clear my name? Will you tell my ma what I've been up to? I'd hate for her to forever think of me as a traitor."

That was the hardest thing anyone ever asked of me. Not because it'd be difficult to do, but because it meant my friend was gone. I wouldn't say yes. Instead, I said, "When this war is over, you'll tell your mama yourself that you were a spy this whole time. Imagine her reaction then."

Mr. Crosby smiled at that. Then, I watched as he rode away on Moon.

As luck had it, Johnny Whitaker came up the drive as Mr. Crosby left.

"What are you doing here?" I asked. There wasn't school today. It was too early for our afternoon ride.

"That shoemaker is here again?"

"He just left."

"You needed *more* shoes?"

I shrugged.

"Seems silly to me that he was back so soon."

"You're the silly one," I said, realizing it wasn't my strongest retort. I bit my lip, not only because of my weak response, but because even Johnny Whitaker found it strange a shoemaker came to our home twice in a short amount of time. If he had noticed, no wonder Mr. Crosby was found out. And did that mean Papa's spy ring was found out in general? I thought we'd been careful. Apparently, we'd need to be even more careful from now on.

∾

Papa handed me a musket. It was heavier than I'd expected and, at first, my arms drooped. I'd seen one before, of course I had. Papa had a number of them hung one on top of another in his bedroom. We were under no circumstances to touch them.

Yet here was Papa, putting one directly into my hands. In the hands of Rebecca, too. I held the gun like a snake, afraid to move, simply waiting for whatever was to come next. I had cradled a black rat snake at the same May Day celebration where Mama had won her arm-wrestling contest. Johnny Whitaker had pushed the thing at me. I'd taken the snake, so many eyes fixated on me that I couldn't refuse. He let me stand there, watching me, until he released the loudest laugh I'd ever heard and he took it back. The whole time I'd wondered if the thing was going to leave deadly marks. Papa later told me it was nonvenomous and was more of a squeezer than a biter.

"It's not loaded," Papa said now.

Then, he showed Rebecca and me how to change that, beginning by using his teeth to rip open a package of powder charge.

I swallowed. I watched, noticing my next younger sister, Mary, sitting on the fence watching, too. I learned not only how to shoot a musket, but also why Papa had given Rebecca and me guns.

"I'd like you two to patrol outside the house at night, to keep an eye on anyone approaching."

"But Mr. Crosby has left," I couldn't help pointing out.

"Yes, but we don't know for certain where the British assumed him to be. That was never said. So, we'll be on guard in case they come looking for him here."

Rebecca asked, "And if they do?"

"Shoot your gun at the sky," Papa said. "Nothing more than that. My daughters are watchmen, not soldiers. Your mama will already tan my hide for asking you both to do this much. Understood?"

We chorused, "Yes, sir."

That response was expected. But I felt a pang in my stomach, as I wondered yet again why being a girl kept me from being things, like a soldier. Johnny Whitaker would be one soon.

"Good. God willing there'll be no shots. But if there are, it'll bring me outside to handle the situation. That is, unless the situation is scared off."

Papa said it so casually. But the idea of him running out of the house to meet someone trying to capture Mr. Crosby, dead or alive, left me shivering.

It made me remember all those years ago how a mob of Loyalists had hooted and hollered in our woods, before the fireflies came and saved us.

Each night, that feeling and memory stayed with me. I stared out an upper window or hunched behind the barrels on the porch or lay in the tall grass, listening for any deep coughs or a rustling in our trees. I watched for any torches or any movement that didn't belong to a rabbit or squirrel.

Rebecca did the same, with us drawing straws to see who'd get the inside window where it was warm, dry—and safest. She'd won the last three nights in a row. And I had the poor fortune of being on my belly within the grass, piled under my shabby cape and wool blankets, and being the first to know ants had surfaced.

I heard a warble and my heart rate soared, until I realized it came from one of our spies.

*Breathe*, I told myself. *He's a Patriot. He's one of us.*

I stood to greet him, shaking off the ants. Then, I was back on my belly.

I didn't know how to read the moon to tell time, nor had Papa told us for how long each night we'd act as sentinels. So Rebecca and I made a game of it, each vowing to keep our eyes open the longest. Whoever tired first whistled. But we each made sure not to signal defeat until well after Mama had blown out all the house's candles, darkening the outside, too. In this regard, I'd won the last three nights in a row. Star helped. He was tucked away in his barn, but every once in a while, he'd called to me, as if saying *Don't you dare give up first.*

"Don't you worry, boy," I whispered back.

In the mornings, Mama—that sweet soul—let Rebecca and me sleep late into the day. Mary was the third oldest, now eleven going on twelve, and was the newest to be kept home from school to help with our never-ending farm work. She was supposed to help, specifically, with Rebecca's and my share of farm work while we slept.

When we woke, we coded, if there was anything new to code. Then I'd go to say hello to my boy, who generally looked as tired as me. But he wouldn't lag behind as we walked toward the tree line. One day, I'd noticed some big old branches that'd snapped from the trees to the ground. I figured they were water-logged from the winter's snow and the rain we'd had so far.

While I dragged the branches, indeed heavy with water, Star chomped on budding flowers. I quickly eyeballed the plant to make sure they weren't periwinkles or another type of seedling that could hurt him. Papa once hollered at Star when he went exploring near the tomato plants. I hadn't known they could be poisonous to my boy. Since then, I made sure to always check. The flowers were fine, and I gave him a playful smack on his rump. "Thanks for the help."

He nickered a laugh.

"All right, boy." I had the branches in place on the ground, aligned like the rungs of a ladder. "Let's practice."

Holding his rope, I led him through my obstacle. Star high-stepped his way over each log-like branch every time. We did it quicker, and quicker, until he was running, and until he was completing the task with me on his back. "Proud of you," I told him.

The praise went straight to his tail, and it rose, resembling a flag off his rump. A proud horse with a flagged tail only had a mind for himself. I laughed then refocused him, pointing us toward home.

There, Papa had work for Rebecca and me. A new letter had arrived by messenger for us to decode. Papa left us, and we set about figuring out the new message, one that included *476. Harvest*, and left me surmising this note was about timing to dismiss Papa's men to their homes for planting season—nothing damaging like the threat against Mr. Crosby.

I blew out a breath in relief, the exhale immediately followed by a yawn so large it closed my eyes. When Rebecca said, "602," I blinked away my exhaustion and ran my finger down the words I'd painstakingly recorded. At 601, my finger stopped over *Enoch Crosby*.

Was he well? Had he been caught? Where had my friend gone? Surely, we'd have received news if something had happened to him.

With another long exhale, I concentrated one line lower to the number Rebecca had asked for: *602.*

*Colonel Ludington.*

Something in my subconscious flared. It was a tickling sensation. Heat flooded my body. There was Papa's name and on top was Mr. Crosby's.

*601* and *602*.

But in the message about the threat to Mr. Crosby hadn't the number been even? I'd made a specific note of it in my mind, had I not?

That meant one thing. One horrible, crippling thing. I'd been wrong. Deadly wrong. That threat wasn't about Mr. Crosby. The "dead or alive" threat was about Papa. Papa was 602.

# CHAPTER 19

My throat felt swollen, twice … no, triple the size. Since Papa switched sides, the threat of the Loyalists getting some sort of revenge had hovered over us like a rain cloud. It only worsened with him becoming a colonel, then when he became a saboteur.

Now … dead or alive … the Loyalists wanted Papa. Their threats had escalated to a level that left me slack-jawed.

We could survive without crops or even without a cow, but never without Papa. The Loyalists couldn't have him. My eyes pricked with tears.

"Sybil," Rebecca said. "What's 602?"

She was waiting for me to finish decoding the message. But I couldn't—I wouldn't—say Papa's name.

Before, I was the one who hurried, trying to impress Papa and Mr. Crosby, and look what I'd done. I'd sent the wrong man away. And Papa didn't know about the danger to him. I should tell him. But how did I tell him I made such a colossal mistake? Should I simply admit it, say, "Papa, I was careless."

*Careless* didn't feel like a big enough word.

He'd be so disappointed. He had chosen to give me such big responsibility. Papa had trusted me. But he wouldn't trust me anymore. Mama wouldn't either. All she wanted was our safety, and I'd put Papa's in jeopardy.

Papa's response to the threat, though, had been for Rebecca and me to patrol for danger. That was all. He even wanted Mr. Crosby to stay at our house, despite that danger. If Papa knew the threat was actually about him, would he react any differently?

And … the war had already been going on for two years, almost to the day. General Washington's spy efforts had been prosperous. Papa had said as much. The war would be over soon, I convinced myself, and the threat to Papa would vanish.

Until then, I'd simply keep my eyes open. Focused. Alert. Even as I thought it, it felt wrong. But I pushed those feelings down. I'd shrink to half my size if Mama and Papa looked at me with disappointment or anger.

"Sybil," Rebecca demanded. "What's 602?"

I remained static, staring blankly.

She huffed and leaned over to see the codebook.

I held my breath.

Rebecca leaned back.

She repeated the process, finishing the message. "What's your problem? You're acting like a dolt."

I spat, "Am not."

But I was.

She raised an eyebrow. "If you say so. I'm going to go give Papa this letter. By myself."

I exhaled. Rebecca hadn't realized my mistake of switching Mr. Crosby's name for Papa's.

But my mistake wouldn't let me rest. The threat to Papa was looming.

Looming.

Looming.

That afternoon, it took three strides on Star's and Rosemary's backs for Johnny Whitaker to ask me, "What's wrong?"

"Nothing," I muttered.

He pressed. I told him everything was fine.

"Sybil, aren't we friends?"

I smiled at that. As a girl who only left her property on Sundays, it was nice to have a friend. And Johnny Whitaker was a friend.

So I told him.

I told him about the spy ring.

I told him about Mr. Crosby.

In which Johnny Whitaker said, "I knew you didn't get new shoes!"

I shook my head, and I told him about the huge mistake I'd made.

From his horse, his hand closed around my shoulder. His grasp was stronger than I had expected. "I'll keep an eye out. Your papa means a lot to me, too. You mean a lot to me, Sybil."

That part made my cheeks hot. I ignored it and said, "Should I confess?"

His mouth twisted left and right. "It'd be the right thing to do."

I sighed.

"But," he said, "you're patrolling. You'll know if danger is lurking."

Right. Still, my hand shook holding the reins. Guilt. Uncertainty. Fear. I felt it all.

That night, Rebecca's and my nighttime patrol was eerily quiet. I was inside the house at the window. Rebecca was in the tall grass. While Johnny and I were out riding earlier, Papa's regiment had disbanded, all of them leaving the encampment and returning to their farms to plant. There'd be no warbles from them.

The next day, Papa was busy with the start of our own planting season. I freed Star from his pasture, and he followed me around like one of the dogs. Our actual dogs followed my siblings and me, too. We all helped, the whole family, weeding, plowing, tilling. It'd take days, and then we'd wait a few weeks before we lay the seeds. The soil needed time after being disturbed. Whenever possible, I watched the drive, the tree line, the creek for any signs of danger.

There was more work to be done the following day, but I caught Papa trying to saddle Pepper to leave the property.

"Wait," I said, too quickly. I even moved in front of him.

"Sybil?"

I sputtered, "I need help with Star."

Who was fine and dandy eating his midday hay. The farm help and the rest of the family were in the fields. I should've been, too, but I couldn't let Papa out of my sight. If he left our property, a Loyalist could set their eyes on him—and decide to collect that reward of three hundred guineas. That was a lot, a lot, a lot of money.

Papa leaned around me. Of course, Star was watching us, chewing. It may've been the one and only time Star and I were not on the same page. "What's wrong with him?"

My brain came up empty. Until, "He's about to throw a shoe."

"Now?" I watched Papa do the math in his head about how long ago we had Star's hooves trimmed. "Why don't I send word to the farrier when I'm in town. He'll do it tomorrow. Pepper, too."

"But …" I began. "Star seemed like he was having trouble on the rocky ground yesterday when Johnny Whitaker and I did our loop."

I knew Papa wanted me to patrol, but my insides felt slimy at my lie. In truth, Johnny Whitaker and I would be able to do our rounds just fine; Star's shoes had another week or two in them.

Papa relented, and while it didn't take him all afternoon to shoe Star and Pepper, it took long enough where his trip into town had to wait.

I felt guilty and slimy still, but relieved. I felt more relieved than slimy.

Johnny Whitaker, Rosemary, Star, and I patrolled our loop twice. During supper, my siblings carried on, but I was too pre-occupied to join in. As I had every night since discovering my titanic blunder, I glanced too often toward the window, as if expecting to see someone standing there with a musket. There was also the fear that I wouldn't see anyone, but a shot would whizz through the window, aimed for Papa.

*Dead or alive.*

Such a terrifying thought.

And I thought again, *I should tell Papa.*

He looked at me across the table. "How was Star on your ride?"

"Excellent. Thank you for helping us."

Papa smiled at me.

That smile cut into me. I'd tell him tomorrow. Papa's safety was too important not to. Only, it was a shame tomorrow was Star's and my birthday. I'd rather Mama and Papa didn't look at me with utter disappointment on such a day.

He asked, "See anything worth noting out there?"

"No," I said, which was part of why I told myself I could wait until the morning.

"Good," Mama said. "No need for you roaming about on that horse of yours. I worry someone will try to snatch you."

"I know, but I always stay close," I reminded her, as I always did. "And I'm with Johnny Whitaker."

"Mm-hmm," she said into her drink.

"But speaking of patrolling," I said, "Rebecca and I should get started for the night."

It was nearing seven. The sun would be setting soon. If only the fireflies would come. They had before in the springtime when the mob of Loyalists crept into our woods and toward our home. Why not now, when I so badly needed my beetles to show themselves and tell me that Papa wouldn't end up in the hands of our enemies?

"Please come," I whispered to myself as I stood from the table.

Rebecca still had food on her plate, but she pushed it away. Archibald wasted no time pulling it toward him.

As we left, muskets in hand, I heard Mama ask Mary to get Little Abigail ready for bed and for the boys to get the brooms and dustpans to clean up their messes.

Tonight, I drew the shorter straw. But Rebecca surprised me by staying outside. She took the porch and I headed toward the tall grass.

Our crazy rooster crowed.

The sky turned a deep red, darkening with each minute that passed.

Mama always liked to recite the rhyme … *red sky at night, sailors' delight*. And I hoped tonight's sunset also forecasted a more positive reaction from Mama and Papa to my confession tomorrow than I expected.

I shivered and repositioned on my elbows.

I searched for the fireflies. Would they come? I needed them. Oh how I needed them to tell me everything would be all right.

Rebecca was humming to herself.

Inside, I heard the commotion of dishes being piled and the high-pitched voices of my brothers. Little Abigail was crying.

That was when I saw them. Not fireflies as I had hoped for earlier. But men. Men slinked through the woods, barely making a noise, right toward us.

# CHAPTER 20

It was more than *men*. It was a horde of them, a mob of Loyalists. Before, when the mob had come, they had been noisy, boisterous. They'd wanted us to know and to be scared. This time, they were eerily quiet. These men didn't want to only scare us. I knew it in my bones; they were coming for Papa and that monstrous reward.

*Fireflies, talk to me, where are you?*

*Show me your magic*, I urged.

*Tell me these men won't hurt Papa*, I begged.

But the night remained dark and still.

Except for the moving shadows of the approaching men.

Closer, and closer they came.

My fingernails dug into the dirt. I searched frantically for a glow of light.

Were they not going to come?

Was I not deserving of the fireflies' magic?

Was it because I created this mess?

I sunk my nails deeper into the dirt.

And now it was up to me to fix it?

There wasn't time to wait for an answer.

I shook out my hands, hoping my nerves and guilt and unease and doubts shook out, too.

I began at a crawl, then I crouched, then I ran toward my sister on the porch.

She startled when I was suddenly beside her.

"Sybil," she hissed. "You scared me."

I used my musket to point into the dark forest, my own gaze following the long barrel. I heard Rebecca's gasp. My gun felt heavy in my hands. I should fire it. It was what Papa had told us to do. Fire it and he'd come running. He'd handle the situation, in this case: his capturers. Or worse: his assassins.

I quivered. I wouldn't fire my gun. That felt like hand-delivering a worm to a bird's nest to be gobbled.

There was a single Papa and dozens of those men.

"No," I said to myself, "don't fire." Then I whispered to Rebecca, "Don't fire your gun."

"What?"

"Don't," I said.

"Why on earth not?"

"Just don't."

I wracked my brain for what to do.

"My goodness," Rebecca hissed. "They're like a small army."

She wasn't wrong. Was my face as white as hers? Fear certainly coursed through my body. I looked behind us at the house, where Papa was, where Mama was, where my brothers and sisters were. Then back at the approaching men. There was so many of them. A small army was exactly what they were. They now moved in groups, in three different directions. One straight at us. One to the left. One to the right. They meant to surround the house. My eyes kept counting, counting, and counting. Fifty. There had to be at least fifty of them.

Then I saw a lone figure, approaching from a different direction. He moved quickly, faster than the approaching mobs.

He ran at a crouch, as I had done, when I didn't want to be seen.

"Johnny Whitaker," I gasped.

"What?" Rebecca said.

"There." I pointed.

In a matter of breaths, he was no longer there, but here. Johnny Whitaker nearly fell into me, panting. "Loyalists. I looped around them to warn you."

"We see them," I said. It was impossible not to.

I peered at the house again, as if I could see through the walls and curtained windows. But I did see the silhouette of two of my siblings behind the window, illuminated by Mama's love of candles. One of my brothers chased the other with what I guessed to be a broomstick.

What if ... the idea began to form. What if we had our own small army?

That broom looked a lot like a musket.

We could scare off the mob. I told myself the Loyalists hadn't come here for a battle. They wanted to take Papa by surprise. I told myself it because I needed to believe it. They wanted to easily capture Papa.

I needed to make them think it wouldn't be so simple and that he was well guarded.

*Misinformation.* Wasn't that the technique General Washington was so fond of using? It had worked for him. It *needed* to work for me, too.

"Rebecca," I whispered. But I didn't say more, I simply pushed her backward, and inside the door to our house. Then, "Get everyone into the parlor."

"What?" she said.

"Do it. Quickly. Johnny," I said, there was no time for his full name. "Help her gather everyone."

We locked eyes. He nodded. Rebecca nodded. I wasted no time to run toward Mama and Papa's bedroom. There were two muskets left on their wall. I cradled them, and my own musket, as I ran to meet my family.

I eyeballed everyone: Mama, Papa, Rebecca, Archibald, Henry, Derick, Tertullus. And, Johnny.

"Where's Mary?" I called, "Mary!"

With me, there'd be ten of us.

Could ten scare off fifty?

Mama said, "Quiet now, Mary's putting Abigail down. Sybil, what is all of this about? Why is Johnny here this late? Why do you have those guns in the house?"

I handed Papa a gun. He took it, his face blank. He had no idea what was going on, but he recognized something was happening. Papa was a soldier, after all. He awaited instruction, patiently.

Mama held zero patience. "Sybil," she snapped. I shoved a gun at her. She hesitated, but she must've accepted the desperation and urgency in my eyes. She took the musket, but still asked, "What in God's name is wrong with you, child?"

I mumbled to myself, "The boys are too short."

I lifted Tertullus, only days from four years old, onto the couch. Instinctively, his knees bent, his head shot in Mama's direction as if waiting to be scolded, awkwardly holding the broom in his hands.

"Sybil!" Mama shouted again.

But I was already lifting Derick. The couch's extra height took him from a tall six-year-old to a gangly sixteen-year-old. By the time I had Derick on the couch, I turned to see Rebecca lifting Henry onto a chair. Bless her.

Not to be left out, Archibald found his own chair to stand on, wearing a sly smile and holding the second broom.

Mary came running down the stairs, confusion written across her face at all the commotion from Mama and me.

Papa said, "Sybil, what is it?"

I paused, panting. "There's a mob of Loyalists outside."

As if waiting for a proper introduction, their voices sprung to life beyond our walls. The men began heckling, telling us they were coming. There was laughter, crowing, cackling.

It launched another wave of fear into me. They no longer cared about taking Papa by surprise. They were announcing *We're coming!*

Papa's head snapped toward the windows. The curtains were drawn, hiding us inside. He took a step toward them and I stopped him with my words: "But I have an idea." Most of the candles were lit. I grabbed one to light the remaining few that must've blown out. "From outside," I said as I ran from one candlestick to the next, "with all Mama's candles lit, the boys look like soldiers. The brooms look like guns. You have a real one, Papa. Mama does. Rebecca does." I handed my gun to Johnny. "Johnny does. Mary," I said to her, "move about. March back and forth."

"Remain behind me," Papa chimed in. He handed her the poker from the fire. "But yes, Mary, march."

He understood my ruse. My misinformation. I had transformed our small family into a small cavalry.

For myself, I took the fireplace shovel.

My heart pounded in my chest as I marched. The threats outside grew louder and closer. They continued to cackle, hoot, and holler. Their shouts sounded so much like they had before that my grip loosened on my sham gun. I squeezed my fingers tighter.

Papa returned their war cries. The boys joined in. Us girls did, too, deepening our voices. Mama may've been the loudest. We sounded crazed, angry, like we were going to war.

We were, to save Papa. Except, my family didn't know that. I had deceived them and put us all in harm's way. Mama marched, like the rest of us, but her eyes flicked to the stairs, where Little Abigail was above us, no doubt crying. I couldn't hear her because of all the hullabaloo.

My own eyes blurred with tears.

Papa motioned for us to be quiet, to listen.

Our room went silent, after one final hoot from Archibald.

Abigail was crying upstairs, but the noise outside had stopped.

Papa rushed toward a window, moving aside a sliver of the curtain. "They're retreating," he said. "They're leaving. We've scared them off." From one face to the next, Papa looked at us all, as if counting his blessings. Mama dropped her musket and ran toward the stairs and Little Abigail.

Papa's big hand circled the back of my head. With his other hand, he took my musket. "Thank you, Sybil," He pulled me into his chest and squeezed.

He squeezed the tears right out of me. "Don't thank me," I said. "Never thank me. This is all my fault."

# CHAPTER 21

I confessed.

Then, I stood there, one hand in the other.

Papa's expression didn't give anything away. Nor was I the first person he addressed. It was Rebecca. "Take your brothers and sisters into the cellar," he told her.

She began herding them away. They moved reluctantly, probably not wanting to miss whatever I had coming.

"Johnny," he said. "You should go underground, too."

Johnny met my eyes and he mouthed, *good luck*.

Outside, the mob began their noises again. That got my sisters moving. I tensed, afraid they'd come back, afraid my ruse wouldn't work a second time.

"It's the wind," Papa said, "making them sound closer. But they're deep in the grove. They've lost the element of surprise. They won't come back. Not likely, anyway. But my guess is they'll taunt us until sunrise."

"I'm sorry, Papa."

"For the men coming here?"

"No, for not telling you as soon as I realized they could be coming. For you."

"It's not me I worry about."

The men outside echoed my confession shouting the name

*Ludington* instead of *Crosby*. They were never after Mr. Crosby. I doubt they even knew he was a spy. I doubt they knew Papa was a spy ringleader. It was simply that Papa was a thorn in their side they wanted to remove.

"Now, why was Johnny here?"

I cringed. I messed up about that, too. "I told him about our spy ring and then how I got the codes wrong. He saw the men and came here to warn us."

Papa turned his head away from me, hiding his expression. Maybe it was for the better. A vein in his neck bulged, telling me all I needed to know.

Mama came down then, holding Little Abigail asleep on her shoulder. My little sister's cheeks were rosy red. Papa asked her to wait in the cellar with the rest of our family. Mama's regard jumped from Papa to me and back to Papa. She left.

Papa finally looked at me. And, yes, he was angry. "You could've jeopardized everything we've done by telling Johnny."

"I'm sorry, sir."

"I know you are." He pressed on his temples. "I suppose Johnny proved himself worthy of knowing. Funny, his father is one of my spies."

My mouth fell open. I hadn't seen him among the spies that came to our house.

"He's a new addition," Papa said, as if sensing my confusion. "I sent him off this morning to scout for me. All my farmers are busy."

Papa's tone didn't sound as angry now. I asked in a small voice, "What are we going to do?"

"*We*," Papa said, "aren't going to do anything." His gaze was hot on me again. I felt fevered from all that happened tonight, as if I was about to begin swaying on my feet. "Go join the others."

I didn't want to listen. I wanted to remain with Papa and fix what I'd started. But this wasn't the time to be bold. The time to be bold was yet to come. For now, I went underground with the others.

∾

The mob taunted us until daybreak, just as Papa had said they would. I slept little, on account of the various whines of my brothers and sisters, the cramped quarters, the chill, the dampness, and the plain old fact that I was worried about Papa upstairs, with the rest of us safely down here.

If that wasn't enough, Johnny Whitaker felt the need to taunt me, too.

"You called me Johnny last night," he whispered in the dark. "First time ever."

"It's your name isn't it?" I asked impishly. But I knew what I'd done.

I sensed his smirk, even if I couldn't clearly see it. "Well, can I stay *Johnny*?"

I smiled. "I suppose."

Mama quieted us with a *shh*.

In the morning, Papa informed us the mob was long gone. The whole time, Mama hadn't said anything to me, beyond that shushing noise. But sometimes silence could be very loud.

A letter arrived in the morning. Not mailed, but delivered by messenger on a horse. Urgent news was delivered this way. When the messenger removed his boot to retrieve the letter, we knew it was urgent *and* clandestine news.

It informed Papa that there was a large group of Loyalists in the area.

We could have told the messenger that. Even Johnny could've, being he was the first to see them. Johnny went home, his own mama probably worried sick, and the entire family sat around the breakfast table, nearly falling headfirst into their bowls and plates.

But, the letter came with added information. A man named Ichabod Prosser, a notorious Loyalist, led the group. Their encampment was thirty miles away and, while on their way to the British headquarters in Manhattan, they thought they'd stop here and claim the bounty for Papa.

How convenient for them.

When Papa got done relaying the message to us around the breakfast table, he added, "At least we know Crosby is well. And I'll write to inform him he's not the wanted man."

"What do you mean he's well?" I choked out.

"The letter was signed *EC*."

A smile appeared as quick as a wink. So he was well, and still spying.

Papa slid the letter toward me. "He also wrote something at the bottom."

The corner of the paper caught something spilled on the

126

table. The wet spot grew, but I saw what Mr. Crosby wrote before it smeared.

*P.S. Hbd, SL*

He'd written a code, for me. Well, not in actuality a code, but an abbreviation.

*P.S. Happy birthday, Sybil Ludington*

My friend thought of me.

I needed that today, on a day where it seemed like Mr. Crosby would be the only one to acknowledge the occasion. Though, he'd forgotten about Star. I wouldn't tell my boy.

Like before, my horse followed me about the grounds, and my family lumbered through the morning turned afternoon. Today's farming focus was the cornfield. Our plow horse, Jasper, would help there.

Mama still hadn't said a word to me about my blunder.

I felt heavy and tired as I led Star to a water trough. He lowered his head and began sucking up a drink. A cloud formed above us, making the already cool day even cooler. I retied my worn cape around my neck.

At a second trough, Papa brought Jasper. He was in mid conversation with Mama. "They'll be in Manhattan a while."

Mama sniffed the sky. "Rain is coming."

"They won't be back tonight."

"No, but another group of men? Another night? You're still a wanted man, Henry."

Papa didn't have an answer for that, beyond, "We'll be watchful as we always have. It's all we can do."

Thank goodness. That meant Rebecca and me. Papa still

needed me. I had to be enough to keep him safe. He glanced at me then, and nodded in a "yes, you were meant to hear that" manner. And in my mind he was also saying, *"You made mistakes, but those mistakes are behind us."*

The timing would've been perfect if the sun poked through the clouds then. It didn't. But my sister did pop up beside me, her voice in my ear. "I have something for you."

I nearly jumped out of my skin and Star pranced beside me, equally startled. "Something for me?"

"Come on," Rebecca said, and the three of us went toward the barn, Mary calling to us, "Where are you going?"

But Rebecca only said, "We'll be back."

Behind an old barrel she revealed something blue. The one something became two. She held out the blue fabrics to me.

"What's this?"

Star nosed the neatly folded cloths.

"Here." Rebecca took one and shook it out. "A new saddle blanket for Star."

I shook out what I held, too. It was a deep blue cape, at least three times the thickness of the worn one I currently wore. "You made these?" She'd always been better in the sewing room than me.

Rebecca smiled shyly. "For your birthdays."

My nose pricked with emotion. "When did you even have time?"

She shrugged. "You sleep longer than me."

At that, I laughed, and pulled my sister into a hug. It wasn't something we did often and it was easier to say, "Thank you," while my face was hidden.

Perhaps it was also easier for her to be honest with me when she likewise couldn't see my face. "I wanted your day to be special, even if just a little. It can be hard in a family so large to have something of your own. It's easy to be overlooked."

When our hug ended, Rebecca's gaze jumped to Star.

I offered, "How about we all go for a ride?"

"Really? But you've never—"

"It's about time you rode him."

She asked, "Can we do your loop?"

We could.

And we did, my sister on the saddle and me sitting behind her, my backside quite comfortable on the new blanket she'd made for Star. We rode amongst the trees, along the stream, toward Papa's empty encampment, through Ludingtonville, giving Johnny a wave as we passed his house, and back again. After the scariness of last night, it was comforting to have my sister with me, in case any of the men lingered. But all was quiet and well.

And, what Rebecca had said in the barn stayed with me like the quickening breeze, about how, in a family as large as ours, it was easy to be overlooked. I wondered if she'd meant how easy she, specifically, was overlooked?

Star was mine. I'd made him all my own. But what did my sister have that was all her own? Just then, she said to me, twisting in the saddle, "If I have to be in anyone's shadow, I'm glad it's yours, Sybil. That's what I wrote that day, back when Papa was showing us the invisible ink."

I remembered that moment, wondering what secret she was too reluctant to reveal. All this time, I'd been fighting with my sister for attention, wanting to outdo her. But I had it all wrong about Rebecca. She had never wanted to overshadow me. My sister only wanted something for herself, too.

She faced forward then, and I lay my head on her back. Not even a breath later, it was as if the clouds split open.

Mama was right about the rain. And boy was it cold. But still, my sister and I laughed at how sudden it came on.

It felt good to laugh.

Now was the time for such things.

Papa may've been certain last night's mob wouldn't return, but there were more men out there who could be a threat. It wouldn't be long before Mama was right about that, too.

# CHAPTER 22

The month of April continued with the promise of three unwelcomed things each day:

Rain.

Papa as a wanted man.

Mama's silence.

Though, to be fair, Mama spoke to me. She just didn't talk to me. There was a difference. Her speaking was merely directional.

*Collect the eggs. Mend this. Quiet your brothers.*

Rebecca insisted, as we were baking a sugar, cinnamon, and nutmeg birthday cake for Tertullus, that Mama was only worried about Papa's safety and it was spilling over onto me.

I thought it was more than that, and I wanted Mama to trust me again, beyond fetching water. Even performing that task, I felt her watching me, making sure I didn't spill too much on my way inside from the well. In truth, the rain refilled anything I spilled. While the rain was good for the seeds we'd put into the ground, it was otherwise a relentless nuisance, especially while Rebecca and I guarded the house and when Johnny and I did our loop of the property.

Since Ichabod Prosser's mob, no one else had stepped foot on our land—that we were aware of, at least. What scared me was that Papa wanted to step foot off of it.

It was the first day in many where it wasn't raining. Mama woke us up by nine to make the most of the sunshine. While I ate breakfast, Mama and Papa's conversation turned hushed. I took notice of what they were saying then, when Papa said he was taking Pepper out.

"Abigail," Papa said. "I'm their Colonel. It's my duty to ride out and canvass the area."

I wrung my hands, and imagined I wouldn't stop until his head bobbed with each up and down of Pepper's trot over the hill and back toward our house.

Mama crossed her arms, but her eyes gave away her concern. "And what if you come across those Cowboys or other Loyalists when you're out there all by yourself? Then what? What will you do?"

Papa thought on it, tapping his spoon and turning over an idea like our mill turned the large waterwheel. Then, "I'll bring the muskets and the girls with me."

Mama snapped, "You will not."

"There's no one else, unless you want me to bring Archibald."

Mama's nostrils flared. "Don't get smart with me. We both know he's too young."

Papa said while chewing, "Well, all the farmers are busy on their lands."

"What about Johnny or his papa? They know all of our secrets anyway."

I slumped down in my seat at the mention of my friend.

Papa swallowed and sipped from his water. "Whitaker has a backlog of work at the mill and Johnny is helping over on Ernest's farm. I even tried to get Johnny to help here but he was already snatched up."

Mama groaned.

Papa got his way. We'd be going with him as he canvassed the area.

He rushed our food into our mouths and then he handed Rebecca and me our muskets. He asked me to saddle Star. He put Rebecca on Pepper, who tried to shake her off until Papa climbed up, too.

Then Papa said, "It'll be like your nightly loop, Sybil, but larger."

Much larger. My route took an hour or so, and we trotted much of the way. For this loop, we'd walk. And for this loop, Papa informed us it would be forty miles, when all the miles were heaped together.

My eyes turned into saucers. Forty miles was over a week's worth of Star's and my normal rides. I closed my eyes, doing the math of how long it'd take. Likely ten hours. I'd never sat on a horse that long. I'd never sat that long, period.

We began on the ox-cart road, except Papa took us south. When going to school, I'd always been taken north. Also, never before had I brought a musket on one of my rides.

I wasn't holding the gun. It was attached to Star's saddle. But it was loaded. I worried it'd somehow go off, hitting Star or taking off a portion of my leg or foot. But more so I was worried about us having to actually use the guns and the gunshot's roar spooking Star. Any time Papa shot while hunting, he took Pepper, and Papa only fired from the ground, never mounted.

I glanced at Rebecca, whose face showed less worry. But that was customary of her. Rebecca was the kind of girl who had both feet on the ground, even when suspended from a horse.

We rode on and on, at a slow cadence, dense trees flanking the trail. The pace itself was calming, and I felt myself easing into the novelty of being off the farm, away from the noise, and a break from Mama's silence. With it being planting season, we didn't come across another soul for some time. When we did, I held my breath, Papa lowered the brim of his hat, and we went by the man like we didn't have a care in the world.

Nothing came of it.

Most men and women and children were on their farms. While passing their properties, Papa raised his hat in a hello. The same went for the hamlets and the small villages that we ambled our way through.

Again and again, Papa assured us, "All looks sound. No signs of lawless groups. Barely any fresh tracks in the mud. Nothing for your Mama to bite her nails over."

Hallelujah for that.

Birds paced with us, flying ahead to a low branch, singing, waiting for us to catch up, and then flying ahead to wait again. They seemed to know where we were going before Papa even did.

One hill we came upon was so large that I mentally earmarked it for wintertime sledding. It was ideal, with only a few trees to avoid. What wasn't ideal was that Mama wouldn't ever let me go without Johnny. But soon, even being alone with Johnny wouldn't be allowed, now that I was approaching marrying age. There'd always be a man watching over me. I bet Catherine the Great didn't answer to a man. As it was, Papa told me she'd all but stolen the throne from her husband.

At some points during our loop, we all dismounted and walked alongside Star and Pepper to give them a break. At a lake, we stopped to water our horses and have a bite to eat.

That was when I fully relaxed, while Papa gave us a silly test. While we sat on stumps, his face lit up and he told us to say the following without our tongues slipping up:

*The skunk sat on a stump and thunk the stump stuck, but the stump thunk the skunk stunk.*

At first, with a roll of my eyes, I deemed it too childish. But Rebecca tried, so I of course had to as well. And I threw up my hands each time.

Rebecca and Papa laughed.

But it wasn't as if Rebecca could say it cleanly either.

We both stunk it up.

Papa insisted he could only do it because he had years of practice. He was nearing forty, so lots of years.

As we continued our loop, nearly done, every once in a while, one of us would randomly say *skunk stunk* and we'd all hoot.

It was a good day.

It remained good, even knowing I'd be sore tomorrow and even after Mama saw us coming over the hill and turned on her heel to go inside without greeting us. Did she see, from even that distance, that we were covered in mud?

"She'll come around," Papa said. "Your mama's heart is so big that sometimes it does all the thinking."

Mama was usually a woman of few words, but a handful of days went by and her heart must've still been thinking hard because she hadn't yet progressed from speaking to me to talking to me. Mama gave Papa the same treatment now, too, since he had taken Rebecca and me along for his ride. I couldn't think of a time when I'd disappointed Mama this much before. It weighed on me, like getting stuck out in a rainstorm, my clothes heavy and clingy.

Tonight the rain hammered on our roof like it was doing everything within its power to come inside. After we supped, Rebecca and I delayed going outside to our posts and first played a strategy board game called Nine Man's Morrice in the parlor. Mary had her chin on the table at the board's center, watching Rebecca and me take turns. She yawned. Frankly, I was surprised Mama hadn't sent her to bed.

Soon, the downpour sounded like hooves on our gravel road.

Papa was on his feet in an instant.

"A rider," Papa said.

I dropped my game piece to the board.

The downpour *was* hooves on our gravel road.

"Henry," Mama breathed and clutched her sewing to her chest.

"One of ours," Papa assured her.

By the time the rider was off his horse, Papa had the door open. "Come in. In."

The doorway only showed the night's darkness, the raindrops reflecting orange from the lamplights, until the man stumbled into our home. He was as wet as a fish.

"Mary," Mama said. "Towels."

Off she went running.

The man stood there, labored for breath, dripping, his nose and the tips of his ears beat red.

"Out with it," Papa said. He licked his lips. "Once you are fit to speak."

The man nodded toward the fire, water dripping from his hair and nose.

"Of course," Papa said.

There, the man warmed himself and found his voice. "Danbury. It's on fire, under siege by the British. Two thousand of them. I was sent for your militia."

"My militia?" Papa cursed under his breath. "My militia has disbanded for the season. They're all over the countryside, all four hundred of them."

The man said with urgency, "Then they must be mustered. By daybreak, you must be gathered and marching south."

Papa pinched the bridge of his nose. Mary returned, but

delayed at entering the room, sensing the unrest. The messenger swayed on his feet, exhausted from his efforts from Danbury to our home. How far was it? Papa had shown us the loop we'd done on a map. Danbury was farther to the south and to the west. At least twenty miles.

"Your horse?" Papa asked.

"Too tired. I pushed him hard for over three hours."

"And you?" Papa said.

The messenger was slow to reply, "I can try riding more, with a fresh horse."

Papa paced. "No, it's too far. And, you don't know the route." Papa stopped. "I'll go."

"Then, sir," the messenger asked, "how will you lead your troops? No man would have the strength to do both."

Another expletive slipped from Papa's lips. Mama said, "Girls, upstairs. Now."

Rebecca and I jumped to our feet. We exchanged glances, panic on both our faces. We both knew the British had to be stopped. But this man couldn't muster the troops. Papa couldn't.

I said, "Rebecca and I will go."

# CHAPTER 23

I had volunteered my sister and myself to ride through the rain and the dark and the forty-degree night, without our Papa, for forty miles, with the dangers of any hungry animals and any lurking Loyalists.

I had volunteered my sister and me to do the same feat Mr. Paul Revere had done, but our ride would be three times the distance and he was twice our ages.

I swallowed and set my eyes on my sister, to gauge her reaction to my saying we would accomplish such a feat. What would it be? Doubt or fear? She had a lot to doubt, beginning with her lack of experience on a horse. Or, would Rebecca show a quickness to please our papa? Mirth at being included in my plan?

Rebecca, for once, was slow to step forward. But then she did, and her voice didn't quiver. "Yes, Sybil and I want to help."

"No," Mama bellowed. "Absolutely, completely, unconditionally no. They're only girls! It's too dangerous."

I wanted to respond with anger, to scream, to yell back that Rebecca and me being girls had nothing to do with this. Instead, I took a steadying breath, and said, "No." That was a risky word to say to Mama. "This task would be dangerous for *anyone*, but we completed the same ride only days ago. We know the way. Johnny doesn't, because I know you're about to suggest him like you always do. But he's never done the loop like us. There's no one else who can do this for Danbury."

"It's lunacy! All of it!" Mama stomped her foot. "By the time the troops are mustered and the men march, a full day will pass. Danbury will be lost. Why go, when it's already too late?"

"Still"—Papa took her hand—"we must try. We must face the British. We must battle with them."

Our Mama didn't agree. I understood. She was a mother. Papa was a soldier. It was who they were at their core, with layers added on top to make Papa a father, too. Mama had other layers, as well, seeping in and adding more to who she was. But at their core, yes, that was who they were. Mother. Soldier. And, Mama shook her head bigly at her children completing such a feat. And I realized that she'd have a similar reaction even if I were a boy.

Papa asked Mary to escort the messenger to the kitchen. He asked Rebecca and me to step out of the room.

We waited in the foyer. I was too nervous to try to eavesdrop on their words. Truth be told, the excitement of the messenger's arrival and his news had pulled the words from my mouth that Rebecca and I would go. But now that those words settled on me, I was scared.

Only Papa emerged from the room. "Get whatever clothing you'll need, then meet me at the barn."

I swallowed. At the same time, Rebecca and I found each other's hands and bounded toward our things. Once dressed, we stared at each other, both in woolen stockings, leather boots, and capes. I was at a loss for whatever else we may need. I, for one, knew my brain was too jumbled to think clearly.

As we ran outside, the rain was so monstrous that we both stopped in our tracks. I kept myself from asking, "What *are* we doing?" because Papa already had the barn lit up. I saw him hustling. This was important to him. Rebecca and I ran for the barn.

Star was stamping his feet. His eyes were large. I ran a shaking hand down his neck and buried my head there. I breathed him in. "It's all right, boy," I assured him. "We have all night to spend together. Let's get you ready."

Meanwhile, Papa readied Pepper with his own saddle, a musket attached to it. Then, he showed Rebecca and me the area map. "I'll go to Ludingtonville and alert there," he said. "Just go straight down the drive and head south."

"Yes, sir," we said in unison.

"Then, ten miles to here," he said, pointing out Lake Gleneida.

We nodded.

Papa highlighted other points for us to remember, along with their distances. We repeated them back, imprinting Papa's words on our lips and brains. Then, Papa stared at us, waiting for our final nods.

Too soon, it was time to begin. I dreaded going back into the rain, but it seemed a silly thing to dread entering it, when I'd spend hours pummeled by it, if the storm should hold that long.

At once, Star began blinking the wetness from his eyes. I climbed onto his back before the saddle could get too wet. My feet brushed my musket—one I prayed I wouldn't have to use—and found the stirrups. Despite what was ahead of me, I felt at home here, on Star. It was a small comfort.

Papa's torch—the oil and the cloth sustaining the flames despite the rain—flickered. He had to put it down to help Rebecca onto Pepper. He always shook, every single time, when someone other than Papa tried to ride him. *Like getting the rain off*, I'd thought before. In this moment, that had never been truer.

We all screamed—Papa, Rebecca, and me—as he tossed her, Rebecca landing hard on the wet ground.

I was relieved when her faced showed repugnance instead of pain as she lay there, on her side, and raised her head and hands from the mud. "I'll try again."

Papa helped her stand, then picked up the torch. "No, my dear Rebecca. It'll do no good." I knew it'd be no better if I tried to mount Pepper. Papa squeezed his eyes shut. He licked his lips. "There's no time …" he muttered. Then Papa looked at me, his hat diverting the rain from his face. His pinched eyebrows and the tightness of his jaw revealed a battle going on inside his head. I knew who warred: *Papa the Soldier* and *Papa the Father*. Then, he circled Star, coming to my other side and stretched his arm toward the gravel drive. His halo of torchlight illuminated the first ten feet I'd go. "Can you ride alone?"

Alone?

*Papa the Soldier* had won. I understood why; Papa needed someone. Papa needed *me* to ride. I had ridden alone, those midday rides Papa asked me to do. But those rides were on our property. Those rides were shorter. Even Mr. Revere had ridden with two others, for a stretch of his ride.

But alone, for the entire time, and for so long? Was I capable of such a feat? Surely, that feat would make Papa proud. It'd help our cause. It was what was expected of me. "Yes," I said.

"All right, then. On your way."

Rebecca shifted her weight. My eyes fell on her. She stood there, literally in my shadow cast by Papa's torch. She said nothing, so much like Mama in that way.

Mary raced from the house and reached up to where I sat on Star. "From Mama."

It was a small parcel of food.

Mama stood in the house's window, lit by candlelight, her expression blank, her hand pressed over her chest.

My heart beat with so much punch that I thought it might escape from my body.

Papa squeezed my hand where I fisted Star's reins. "Trust no one, Sybil. Do not get off your horse. Stay on the path. You can do this."

I could do this.

Then, Star and I began our ride.

# CHAPTER 24

Within steps, Star and I left Papa's halo of torchlight. We'd run down this road so many times before that I'd lost count, but this was the first time we'd ever moved this fast.

In the darkness, we passed the barren cornfields, where their seeds were still beneath the ground. Then, we ran along the creek. I saw it all from memory, more so than with my eyes. We were moving too quickly. It was too dark. The gravel drive turned to dirt as Star and I reached the ox-cart road.

It'd be the very first time I'd ever gone on this road alone. "Egad," I said to myself as I made the turn. We went to the left, toward the south, just as I had with Papa and Rebecca. I almost wished Papa had wanted me to go to Ludingtonville. I imagined Johnny's face—in complete awe—as he answered his door and saw what I was doing.

I pushed Star, harder and faster. My cape billowed out behind me, the rain soaking my belly. It was fitting Rebecca had stitched me a dark blue cape. Blue was our color. The British wore red.

Star's breath and exertion was all I heard, beyond my own pulse pumping in my ears and rainfall battering the trees.

Papa needed us. General Washington needed us.

What an honor.

A willowy branch caught the side of my head. It missed my face, a victory in and of itself. A strand of hair had escaped from my braid. I tucked it behind my ear and returned to Star's reins.

I gripped them, tightly. I realized how tightly. And I realized that Star had been galloping for a few minutes now.

"Whoa," I said to him.

My excitement had gotten the better of me. I didn't want to exhaust Star within the first miles. Horses were built to go far, but three miles at a gallop could wipe out a horse's energy. A trot was different. If Star trotted, with a walking break here and there, he could go five times that distance without hurting him. Trot, walk, trot, walk, and so on, in fifteen-mile increments, completing that pattern nearly three times until I reached forty miles. I'd have to guess the timing.

But that was my plan.

We trotted.

Against the cold and rain, I shivered and repositioned my cape to better cover my body, no longer flapping in the breeze. But our slower pace also put our surroundings into greater focus. The world was no longer a blur. It now showed a man-shaped tree here and a bear-shaped shrub there.

"We're all right, Star. Nothing out here but us."

Of course, a wolf or coyote or some beast of considerable size that made considerable noise howled at that moment.

"Just telling his friends we're also in the woods. That's all."

That had to be all.

The first village along my route was near Lake Carmel. We jogged closer and closer. An owl hooted. The trees rustled.

"The rain and wind," I said aloud.

A speck of candlelight showed through a window ahead. I was giddy as we approached, my first stop on completing my feat. I stopped myself from pushing Star faster. At the first home, I nearly dismounted, then remembered Papa's words never to get off Star.

From a tree, I broke a branch.

I stayed on Star's back and, at the first door, I thwacked the stick and called out how the British were burning Danbury and how Colonel Ludington was mustering troops.

A man appeared, still dressed. He hadn't yet gone to sleep. I immediately recognized him as one of Papa's spies, Mr. Wilson. I wasted no time to repeat, "Muster at Colonel Ludington's!"

Mr. Wilson took a step back, at seeing me high on a horse. "Sybil?"

"Yes," and I quickly explained all I knew and how his family should abandon their house if the British should come this way. "Tell the others. Then go to my homestead. Understood?"

I was certain this man wasn't used to taking orders from a child, even one he knew to be his Colonel's daughter. Not even a son, but a daughter. Yet he understood his need to hurry and obey. He even said, "Yes, thank you, Patriot."

*Patriot.* It was the first time I'd ever been directly called that title, even though I'd been acting as one for months.

Renewed excitement filled me. "Ho!" I said to Star and made a clucking sound with my tongue as I pulled on the right rein, taking us in that direction.

I heard Mr. Wilson's movements behind me, then his pounding on his neighbor's door. I continued on, until I came to the final home in the village. I repeated my instructions there, figuring the first and last house in this strip of homes would serve my purposes to tell those in between and the farmers nearby.

My first two stops had been a thrill. I imagined Papa's praise, "Well done, Sybil," especially as I looked over my shoulder and saw the aftereffect of my alerts. Men scurried about, lit by their torches, shouting and informing all within their small village.

As my eyes adjusted to the darkness again, every bone in my body wanted to urge Star into a gallop, but I kept him at a walk to let him suck in air and rest his muscles. There was a hamlet not far off. We'd be there in no time, we'd alert there, then Star and I would trot once more, doubling our pace. We were unstoppable.

# CHAPTER 25

I recognized the next lake as Lake Gleneida. With my stick, I beat on the doors of the hamlet there. "Muster at Ludington's!" I yelled, again and again.

This destination put Star and me at ten of our forty miles, a quarter of the way there. I pictured one fourth of Papa's four hundred militiamen running or riding through the woods. Surely, despite it being nearly midnight, every animal from squirrel to bird was now awake from the commotion one hundred men made as they spread the news and raced toward my home. The first man—hopefully men—had probably already arrived.

The busyness of my mind was a wonderful distraction from the darkness, the rain, the coldness, the unknowns beyond the short distance my eyes could see. I'd stop next in Mahopac. From Papa's map, I remembered the distance being a great stretch from the hamlet of Carmel where I'd last alerted.

The stretch unnerved me, nothing but woods in between, a half-hour of my heart racing in my chest. As a distraction from my quickened heartbeat, I counted Star's two-beat trot.

One, two, one, two, one, two.

First beat: right front hoof, left hind hoof

Second beat: left front hoof, right hind hoof.

I raised up and down from my saddle every other beat.

I blew out a breath. It wasn't cold enough to see the puff of air, but the chill seeped beneath my cape and my dress, making my body begin to ache from shivering. My stockings were soaked through. Rain hadn't ceased to drip from the tip of my nose for the past hour.

If I kept up my trotting and walking, I'd be home within five more hours.

Thirty minutes to Mahopac.

"Keep going, boy. Keep going."

I wiped wetness from my eyes—and that was when I saw the outline of a man. No more than twenty paces ahead. Right there on the trail.

"Whoa," he said in a loud voice.

I stiffened on Star's back.

"You're the girl?" the man called out. "The one alerting about Danbury?"

"Yes," I called.

Then I said my own "Whoa" to Star. We were getting too close to this man too quickly. He didn't wear a British uniform, but he also didn't wear ours. Many of Papa's regiment didn't wear a uniform, though. They wore whatever they had on. This man had on a ragged-looking hat, coat, breeches, and stockings. He didn't have a weapon that I saw, but a firearm or knife could be tucked somewhere on his body.

Papa said to trust no one.

I tightened my grip on my stick. I had my loaded musket, too. Not that I knew how to fire it beyond pointing the barrel at a target and squeezing where I was supposed to squeeze.

"I worried about you," the man said, "out here all on your own."

He worried about me? Did I know this man?

I asked, "Are you in the Colonel's regiment?"

The man took too long to respond. Too long mustering a response, when he should've been mustering at my homestead if he was indeed in Papa's regiment. He finally said, "I thought you could use my help."

He took giant steps toward me.

Too close, entirely too close.

Star snaked his head, lowering his nose and waving his neck from side to side. I'd only seen Star act that way a single time, when a wolf had come sniffing near his pasture.

Was this man my own wolf?

"We aren't in need of any aid," I said. "If you'd move aside so we can pass, I have a task to do."

But he didn't step out of the way. He took another step closer.

"Fine, if you'd like to help," I began, trying to keep the nerves from my voice, "then help by alerting the people of Brewster."

That village wasn't part of my loop, yet it was on the way to Danbury.

The man considered. He stepped again. "I could ride with you," he said.

I shook my head. I opened my mouth to assert a no, but no words came out.

With one more step and an outstretched arm, the man tried to take hold of my reins.

Star snapped his teeth. I swung my stick, barely missing the man. He stumbled, slipping off his feet and into the mud.

I found my voice to call, "Ho!" to Star.

I called it over and over, my voice barely more than a sob. We galloped.

"Trust no one," Papa had said.

I ran us as fast as Star could go.

# CHAPTER 26

A branch sliced my face. I felt a trickle of wetness, mixing with the wetness already on my skin. I closed my eyes and let Star carry me far, far away from the man, whoever he was. Everything in my gut told me he was foe, not friend.

Star and I didn't stop until the woods opened up at the hamlet of Mahopac. I'd pushed Star too far, too long. I immediately dismounted, dismissing Papa's rule to never get off Star's back, along with a niggling sensation that I was safer on Star than on the ground. But I needed to rest him. Fortunately, while his nostrils flared for air, he didn't seem in distress.

He'd be fine, but we'd need to walk instead of jog.

I led him to the first house. I hesitated; weary after my encounter with the man. Anyone could be out here. Anyone could be standing on the other side of each door. I reminded myself that I was needed, and that Mama and Papa were giving me a dose of freedom—a feeling I'd chased for so long that it almost seemed dreamlike to have it now. There would be no giving up.

I knocked. A woman answered, holding a candle in a tray. I let out a small breath at seeing a woman instead of a man. Her eyes went wide at the sight of me. "Child," she gasped. "You're bleeding and soaked to the bone."

I touched my face. "Danbury," I said. "It's burning. I'm mustering the troops for Colonel Ludington."

She called over her shoulder for her husband. He approached, already reaching for his musket. "I heard her," he said. "Who are you, child?"

"Sybil Ludington. Colonel Henry Ludington's daughter, sir. His militia is to meet at headquarters to march at daybreak."

His wife bunched her apron and reached for my face, her head shaking in astonishment. The man only said, "I'll leave at once."

I said, "Tell the others here," and I stepped back, thwarting the woman's attempt to dab at my face. But I offered her a smile before I began leading Star away into the night, the rain more drizzly than soaking now.

The hamlet of Mahopac marked the very bottom of my loop. From there, I began to turn us north instead of continuing south, walking beside Star instead of riding. We stayed this way for the next mile or so. It took precious minutes and my head was on a swivel the entire time. But my boy meant the world to me and I remembered the next stretch to be covered in muddy hills. Star would need his energy.

At the crest of the first hill, I wiped my eyes, tucked the hair that'd come loose from my braid behind my ear, and realized the rain had mercifully stopped. The clouds had even thinned, showing the faintest hint of the moon.

I smiled. We were roughly at my halfway point. I hoped this meant the worst was behind me as I climbed onto Star's back.

And we rode, to Kent Cliffs, stopping to alert there with no incident, then onward toward Farmers Mills. That hamlet presented a challenge for me. Not because of man or beast, but because of its location. If I turned Star to our right, cutting straight through the circle my loop created, I'd be home within half an hour. However, to complete my loop, to keep going north before I could go south again, and before I arrived home, would take three times as long.

It was tempting. Oh, how tempting to cut across the loop. I was three-fourths of the way, having alerted three hundred of Papa's four hundred men. I wished it were good enough. But I had a duty to Papa—and to myself—to complete the full route.

I pushed us north, toward the hamlet of Stormville. That'd be the point where I turned us south again. I yearned for Stormville. I wanted nothing more than to see that strip of homes.

My hands were red. They burned from the cold, from where I gripped the reins and my stick.

My jawline hurt, where my teeth had clenched for so long.

My legs and back and torso ached from keeping beat with Star.

My stomach felt hollow and grumbled for food.

My eyeballs even felt as if they'd been rattled to the point of pain.

I cried out with happiness when we came upon Stormville. "Muster at Ludington's," I called, my voice sounding hoarse, and I banged on their doors. It was well past midnight and they were slower to answer, slower to register my words and jump into action. Irritation filled my voice as I explained that Danbury was under siege. Finally, they understood.

I felt even more exhausted.

We ate then at the hamlet's stables. Star's hay was wet, but Papa once said wet hay was better for a horse anyway. I opened my parcel from Mama to find my favorite meat pie wedged within a shallow mug. I wondered how she was making on at home, what was being done there.

I ate quickly. When I stood, my arms and legs may've been filled with rocks.

*Five miles to Pecksville,* I told myself. Five miles, that was all, to the last town I had to alert. From there, only home was left. Sweet, blessed home, only two miles farther.

"How are you, Star?" I asked him. I picked up one of his hooves and checked his shoe for stuck rocks. I checked his others. With a stick, I dug out packed mud. "All better. Now, what do you say? Can we finish this?"

I twisted my lips at his squeal. The sound he made was short and quiet, but I heard him loud and clear. Star didn't want to leave the barn.

I felt bad leading him outside. While I was urgent to ride him, I walked beside him, stroking his neck, until he calmed beneath my palm. I mounted him then. Each stride brought us closer to Pecksville.

The path here was narrow, more difficult to follow.

I slowed us to a walk, noticing that *something* blocked our way.

It looked like a prone body, but as we inched closer it was no more than a fallen branch.

I advanced Star toward it and he acted, just as we had practiced so many times before, high-stepping over the branch.

I leaned forward to give him a hug. When I sat straight again, Star's one ear flicked back while the other remained forward. His ears usually pointed where we were going. He only ever flicked one back when he heard something.

"You reacting to me, boy? Or something else?"

Was there something behind us?

I twisted to peer into the darkness. I saw nothing. But I heard something. Bells. Cowbells, if my ears didn't deceive me. Most cattle slept outdoors. Ours did. Some grazed, but they mostly slept. Was I near a farm? It was possible.

The chime sounded again, closer.

I almost laughed at myself when I saw the outline of a cow. The night's larks had taken a toll on my mind. But then my mind registered how odd it was for a cow to be on the trail. Then, the cow whinnied.

But cows don't neigh.

Horses did, to say *Hello, is anyone else here?*

Star stamped his feet.

The horse shifted and what I once thought was a branch turned into a man on the horse's back.

The pieces fell into horrifying place. Cowboys were known to lure people by tinkling cowbells. And right now, a band of lawless Cowboys had made me their next mark.

# CHAPTER 27

The Cowboy's horse sidestepped, revealing another portion of the narrow path, and I realized the man wasn't alone. How many were in this lawless band, I couldn't tell. I certainly wasn't about to find out.

I heard the bell again.

No doubt, the Cowboy hoped he'd tinkle his bell and I'd come running. He was right about the running, but not in the direction he had wanted. I was too smart for that. I was a soldier's daughter. I squeezed Star with my heels. He was spooked and wanted to be anywhere but here. It showed in how fast he took off.

The bells were forgotten, now replaced by the sounds of loud clucks, the slap of a whip, and other encouragement for the Cowboys' horses to pursue Star and me. I didn't have the nerve to bring Star to a gallop, not on this path and in this darkness. I held him at a canter. Even that felt daring.

I recognized another fallen branch ahead, this time suspended. We'd need to jump. Could we? We'd done it before, but not at that high of a height. I wasn't certain. And, I'd never been more exhausted. Star and I had covered more than thirty miles of our route, with only a single hamlet left to alert. *If* we could make it there. *There* meant safety, other Patriots to come to our aid.

But first, there was this obstacle. Either we cleared the jump, or we were caught. I wouldn't let my mind fathom what this group would do to me. Star, they'd likely sell to the British. He'd be gone, no longer mine. Tears welled in my eyes, for too many reasons to name only one.

We were mere strides from the log.

Behind me, the men taunted me, calling out crude remarks I'd never dream of repeating. They had recognized me as a girl.

I felt Star reach forward and down with his neck. I leaned into him. Star's front legs, then his hind legs left the ground, but not with his usual strength. We hung in the air. Then we landed. Star's legs bobbled. I dropped my stick and clung to the reins, my butt sliding in the saddle. But I stayed on, at the cost of my foot knocking free my musket.

I twisted to look behind us. My gun lay on the path. The first Cowboy jumped the log. I cursed, repeating the expletive Papa had used earlier. It felt like days had passed since then. The second horse reared, standing up on his hind legs, not wanting to make the jump. The rider fell. The other men and horses in the group began edging off the trail between the close-knit trees and around the fallen log. Three of them? Four? I didn't waste the time to accurately count. Nor did it matter. The closest Cowboy was shortening the distance between us.

I imagined him catching us and pulling me from my horse. Most horses would flee without a rider. But not Star. He wouldn't leave me. He'd be taken, too. When Mr. Paul Revere was captured, they miraculously let him go. They let him walk back to town. But—for me—with those crude remarks spit at my back as they chased me … I shivered. And I pleaded to Star to not lose his footing on the slick ground, to keep going, to not slow down.

But the Cowboy's horse was fresher and the rider himself was bolder.

We couldn't outrun them.

That realization could've knocked me from Star's back. I trembled from fear and from cold. I called out for help. *Anybody! Somebody!*

Pecksville was still too far.

*Think.*

They had brawn, but I had brains.

And there was a break in the trees ahead.

I tugged on Star's reins. We veered between two trunks. Papa had said not to leave the path, but I could lose them this way.

Star slowed, no longer cantering or even trotting, but walking. There was no other way to move deeper into the forest. But we rode through the trees all the time. I knew how to bend, when to lower my body, when to lean to the side. We were quick, gaining distance between them and us.

"Think you'll get away that way, do you?" I heard. But from where? I wasn't sure.

Twigs broke under Star's weight, announcing *here we are!* in the darkness. It was pointless of me, with the other noise we were making, but I held my ragged breath, afraid the Cowboys would hear, until my chest burned, and I feared my lungs would burst. I gulped in air, holding it again.

Star and I twisted through the trees. I looked over my shoulder every couple steps; fearful I'd see a menacing face or hands lunging for me. But I didn't.

We'd lost them.

Still, heckling voices were seemingly everywhere, coming from all directions, but blessedly more distant with each held breath. The wolves chimed in, howling back and forth. They sounded closer than the Cowboys.

I'd take the wolves. I exhaled my breath in relief, at the exact moment Star sunk forward. I nearly went over his head, coming to rest on his wide neck.

He'd stepped straight into a swamp, the water sloshing as he clomped his front feet.

"Oh, boy," I whispered, and I climbed from his back, water halfway up my shins. "What'd we get ourselves into now?"

The whites of his eyes, usually not exposed unless he was scared, caught the moonlight. "Shh, Star, it's all right."

His legs were sinking. We had to hurry.

I stepped farther into the swamp, the water and muck coming to my knees, and waded until I was facing my boy.

I put both hands on his nose and gently pushed. "Back. Easy now. Back."

Star took high steps, inching backward, until he was firmly on hard ground.

I put my forehead to his. "See, we're all right, boy."

But that declaration only brought tears to my eyes.

We were God knows where, with God knows how many Cowboys stalking us, with a wolf pack on the prowl. I listened, for we surely had just made a bunch of noise, but the voices had stopped. Were they lying in wait somewhere? I raised my head and peered around. It was a forest, one tree no different from the next. I had no idea which way to go to return to the trail.

I needed a miracle.

I needed magic.

I needed my fireflies.

They weren't there for me last time I needed them, but would they show themselves to me now? It had rained. Fireflies loved coming out after the rain. But usually that happened in the summertime. It was spring. But I'd seen them before in April. I had.

I closed my eyes. "I believe," I said out loud. "I believe," I repeated, and behind my eyelids I imagined them.

Darkness hit me again when I opened my eyes. My chest tightened. I tentatively led Star forward, still searching for my beetles. I knew I had to find the path, despite the Cowboys maybe being there. From there, I needed courage. A lot of it. Because, all I wanted to do was return home, to see my family, to see Papa's men preparing to march, to let Star rest in his barn, safe and sound.

I wasn't sure I had enough in me to continue on.

Star nudged me with his head, as if saying *Let's go this way*. As if he was saying *We can do this*.

And if I believed in the fireflies, I also needed to believe in Star and me.

We took another step toward where I thought the path could be.

I held my breath once more, this time fighting for composure. I let it out as a sob, a big, overjoyed, beholden sob, because I saw them.

I saw my fireflies.

They'd come.

*We're here* they blinked. *Yes* they said with each spark of light. *The odds are against you. They're against us, too, this time of year. But here we are.*

They flickered again and again.

How magical. How miraculous. How very much a godsend.

I may've been lost and scared and tired, but seeing them reassured me we'd find our way. Star nudged me again. Then, the fireflies did something that released the tears that'd built in my eyes.

They flashed all at once; just as they had for Papa, just as they had for me the night they led me to Star.

"I'm listening," I said softly. What were they trying to say? That I shouldn't give up? That I could complete something as magical as them?

Forty miles, just a kid and her horse, farther than anyone else had gone in a single night.

But we could do this.

*This way* they signaled in unison. *The path is this way.*

If I squinted, a hint of the trail came into view. I began walking faster toward the lightning bugs and that blessed trail, feeling every ache in my legs. Star trailed behind me. They flickered between the trees. By the light of fireflies, Star and I were headed in the right direction once more.

# CHAPTER 28

The fireflies showed me the way. Soundlessly, they blinked, together, in one spot, then they moved to the next, then to the next. I followed, enchanted, until my feet hit the ox-card road again. On the other side was a farm.

It wasn't our farm. Oh how I wished it were. But I recognized it as one of our neighbors and I felt like I could breathe within its vast open space. The rain was gone. The moonlight had fought and won against the clouds. And I knew where to go from here.

In that time, in those short breaths of gaining my bearings, the lightning bugs had moved on. But they had come, showing me with their flickers and flashes that I shouldn't give up.

"Star, we only have a few miles to go." I ran a hand over his star-pattern and down his nose.

He lowered his head, as if saying *Climb on*.

Soon, we trotted into Pecksville. If truth be told, I wanted to trot right through. But the fireflies had given me a gift. I wouldn't waste it. I knocked on the doors. I yelled what I had to yell. The words came out as a croak.

But I spoke them.

And we'd done it. Star and I had completed the arduous

task of alerting four hundred of Papa's militiamen to the British's attack in a single night.

I realized something, too. I once thought the fireflies led me to Star so I could have something all my own. But, without my boy, this moment wouldn't have been possible. It was as if the fireflies knew this night awaited us. The two of us.

All that was left now was the few remaining miles until home. *Home.* That single thought should've been enough of a coaxing, but I began to sway on Star's back. The reins were loose in my hands. It hurt too badly to move my fingers, so I didn't tighten my grasp, nor did I stretch my appendages.

"Skunk stunk," I slurred, evoking Papa and Rebecca in my mind. "Skunk stunk." And again, "Skunk stunk."

Then voices were added to my own. It was the hum of a large group of men. The rooster crowed. I leaned so hard to the left to bring Star from the road to our drive that I nearly fell off. He swung his head, as if saying *Only a little farther now, Sybil.*

The dirt road turned to gravel, crunching under his feet.

We climbed a small hill, the crest of it aglow from the rising sun.

I cried out as Star took his final strides over the hill that blocked us from the house. Then, there it was, the sun turning the outline of my home a deep orange. I saw movement inside. But what was most astonishing was the group of men out front.

There were so many men. And more would be coming from Pecksville.

Some stood. Some sat around makeshift fire pits. Some

tended to their guns. Some ate. Some walked about.

Someone ran toward me.

Rebecca.

She clutched her long dress, holding it above her feet, and she ran for me. "Sybil!"

She called my name again.

It had never sounded so good.

When she reached me, I fell from my horse. Rebecca caught me and softened my way to the ground. Thank goodness my younger sister was taller and bigger than me.

Her arms were around me. "You made it," she whispered.

When she pulled back, I saw her face. Her eyes were tired. Her cheeks were smeared with soot and her clothing was damp. Rebecca's hair had come loose from her braid as mine had.

"Have you been up all night?" I asked.

Rebecca nodded. "There was so much to do."

She had tended to the fires and to the kitchen. She mended clothing and boots. "I even showed Johnny how to load a musket the proper way."

I laughed, just as another somebody barreled into my sister and me.

It was Mama.

She was crying. Mama was bawling. Her heart had never talked to me so clearly and loudly before. But still, in between the sobs, Mama said, "I'm so proud of you. Of both of you."

Papa's arms surrounded us next. But he couldn't stay with us long, just long enough for me to warn him about the Cowboys then whisper, "The fireflies helped me." And for Mama of all people to respond, "God bless those fireflies."

We chuckled at that, just as Johnny joined us.

Papa pulled Mama and Rebecca away, giving me a smile as they left.

Johnny sat down beside me. Star bent, his head between ours.

"Thanks for getting her home safely," Johnny said to him. "You know, Sybil," he said, leaning forward to see me better, "if you keep pulling off nights like that, Paul Revere is going to be the one looking up to you."

"But I'm a girl."

"You're a hero."

I smiled. "And now it's your turn, soldier. Be safe out there."

Johnny rejoined the troop and I took my boy toward the barn. He had earned himself a long nap. With all his horse needs met and a kiss on his muzzle, I stumbled into my own bed. Rebecca was already there. Neither of us bothered to wash up or fully undress. But I had draped my blue cape over the back of a chair. I pictured it billowing in the breeze as Star strode.

Then, I was asleep.

I woke to the sun in my eyes. Rebecca had already left our bed, no surprise there. I padded to our window that overlooked the lawn. Papa, Johnny, and the rest of the militia were gone. If I hadn't seen them with my own eyes, the mass of them at sunrise could've been nothing more than an apparition. Pressed-down grass and circles of blackened dirt were all that remained, where fires had burned through the night to protect them against the cold and rain.

Downstairs, Mary greeted me with a "Finally!"

Our bathing tub sat in the middle of the kitchen. Just Mary and the tub.

"Mama made me keep the water hot all morning," she complained. "Take cooled water out. Put boiling water in. That's what she said to do. Again and again."

All that work, huh? I thought mockingly. But as I sunk my body into that hot water, I'd never been more appreciative of my little sister.

Egad, my muscles were sore.

I wanted to stay in there all day, but Rebecca poked her head into the room. "Still warm?"

It was a novel question for me to consider. This bath was the first one I'd taken since Rebecca was born where I didn't go into the tub last, when the water was cold.

Though, for Rebecca, she'd always been next-to-last. Never second in line. I smiled. "All yours."

As we exchanged places, Mary wore a frown.

"What is it?" I asked.

"You and Rebecca have each other," she said. "The two oldest, practically twins."

"Except I'm taller," Rebecca said with a grin.

"And," Mary went on. "Mama and Papa rely on you two the most."

"Well," I said, "we're the oldest. You said that yourself."

It wasn't the response Mary wanted. I tried, "Mama asked you to help with the bath."

Mary's frown became more pronounced. "Yes, but only because you two were sleeping and you"—she was speaking to me— "can barely move."

I hid a laugh.

"There's the two of you," Mary said. She gestured to herself. "There's me. Then, all the boys, the four of them their own band. It took ten years before Mama had another girl. Little Abigail doesn't even do much yet besides pull my hair. I feel like I have no one. But you two have each other. Your own little band."

I'd never looked at it that way. I'd only ever seen Rebecca as my rival. But maybe we were a team. We worked as one to decipher Papa's codes. We patrolled together. Even last night, I may've been the one to ride into the night, but Rebecca worked just as long preparing the men to march.

I smiled at Rebecca. She smiled right back.

Mary threw up her hands. "See!"

"You're nearly twelve," I said, remembering the year I turned twelve. The year Papa gave me more responsibility. The year I found Star. "It'll be a big year for you, like it was for me."

"Yes," Rebecca said. "Then you can be part of our little band."

"Really?" Mary asked.

"Really," we said.

～

Papa returned a few days later. And, he didn't come alone. I'd be honest, I didn't know who stood next to Papa in our parlor. I'd never seen the man before. Rebecca, Mary, and I sat on the couch, shoulder to shoulder, waiting for his introduction.

The man was tall, but so were we.

He was well dressed. And although he didn't wear a wig like the English did, his hair was powdered white. Papa never did that.

The man, I guessed from the military with his perfect posture, looked older than Papa, too, but not by much.

Papa waited for Mama to enter. She hadn't had a chance to remove her apron yet. He said, "I'd like to introduce His Excellency General Washington."

My mouth dropped open.

Mama turned two shades red and discreetly reached behind herself to undo her apron ties. It was an honor the army's commander in chief was in our home. A great honor.

General Washington's smile was fit for a king. He wasted no time in thanking Papa, bending over Mama's hand—something that made her redden even further—before turning to us children. Rebecca, Mary, and I sat stiff as a board. We'd acted out in front of guests before. We wouldn't in front of His Excellency.

"Which one of you fine ladies is Miss Sybil?"

I stood, locking my knees.

"I'd like to thank you," he said, "for your heroic act as a messenger for our great Continental Army."

I think I reddened just like Mama.

General Washington and Papa, but mostly Papa in his animated voice, explained all that had happened. Even with Papa's militia leaving at daybreak, they hadn't reached the Danbury area until nightfall. Mama had been right—not surprisingly—that it was too late for Papa's men to do anything there. It'd been torched and ransacked. But Papa's men had joined with another militia group and at the next daybreak they'd chased and harassed the British all the way to their ships at the Long Island Sound. Then it was bye-bye British. For that battle, at least.

During Papa's storytelling, Mama looked none too pleased at Papa relaying how they hid behind trees and fences and stonewalls to get off their gunfire or how one man was shot off his horse or how our Colonial men were outnumbered three to one.

"Our numbers were fewer, yes," General Washington said. "But it would've been significantly worse without the Colonel's men. Again, I have you to thank for that, Sybil."

He laid his eyes on me.

I'd been standing the whole time, stuck between knowing if I should've sat again after he'd first addressed me or if I should remain on my feet. So I stood. And now, with those words, I felt myself standing even taller. "I was very pleased that I was able to help in the war," I said.

"You did, indeed, including aiding your father with the other task I bestowed on him." He was talking of the spy ring. "It's a lot to ask of a young person, especially with all your other duties. I was the eldest as well. The oldest of six."

"There are eight of us. *So far*."

I had blurted it out, without thinking. Papa hid a smirk. Mama would spend this entire conversation flushed. General Washington chuckled and said, "You are blessed with a large family."

"I am," I said. Then, I reached back to pull Rebecca to a stand, too. "Rebecca helped Papa as well with your task. We did it together. Then on the night I rode, she singlehandedly helped Mama and Papa to prepare your troops."

"Is that so?" General Washington said turning his focus to my sister. He bowed over her hand, something he hadn't done to me! "I am obliged for your help as well, Miss Rebecca."

I bit back my jealousy to smile for her. I even took a small step backward, so there wouldn't be even the slightest trace of a shadow on my sister.

# CHAPTER 29
### Epilogue

I saw the fireflies often that summer, and the summers that followed. It would take six more years for the war to end and for us to gain our independence from England.

During those years, the lightning bugs didn't always have anything dire to say.

Sometimes their flickers gave me peace, a sign that Papa's safety was intact while he was away with General Washington, serving as one of his aides.

One night, while the fireflies chattered at me, a messenger arrived with a note:

*All is well*

Signed: *EC*

Sometimes the lightning bugs merely said a hello. I always smiled back, remembering the enchanting moments I'd already spent with them, blinking, flashing, and lighting up the night with their flickering.

I hadn't seen them again in the special ways I had before. But I relished in what magic the fireflies had yet to bring. I felt a little of it one night when Mama sat down next to me on the front steps.

She kicked off her shoes and rubbed her feet. She was

pregnant with her eleventh child. My guess, another sister. But that wasn't what I wanted to think about, or talk to Mama about.

The fireflies flickered, as if saying *Go on*.

"Mama," I began, "I don't think the life of a farmer's wife is for me."

Mama stared out at the tree line, beyond it maybe. Finally, she said, "I don't think so either, Sybil."

Her response shocked me.

"You'd be all right with that?"

She smiled and cupped my chin. "It may've taken me time to see it, but you've proven time and time again you're meant to go a great distance."

I leaned my head against her shoulder. "Thank you."

She asked, "Do you know what you want to be?"

She asked it as if I could truly be anything, do anything. But I wasn't sure what I wanted to be. "Not yet," I said, just as I heard a warble. One of Papa's men was headed our way. For now, I had work to do as Sybil the Spy.

# A NOTE FROM THE AUTHOR

Dear Reader,

I hoped you enjoyed experiencing the story of little-known war heroine Sybil Ludington, which was such a spectacular and unbelievable feat that some people believe her midnight ride was nothing more than a story.

But I believe that Sybil accomplished something magical, just like the Sybil in my story believed in the magic of fireflies, and that on April 26, 1777 she truly made this daring ride to warn of an attack by the British.

I added the fireflies because I've always found them to be enchanting creatures perfect for enchanting stories.

The first known reference to Sybil Ludington wasn't until over a century after she completed her ride, in 1880, within a local historian's book. The next mention of Sybil's story appeared in *Colonel Henry Ludington: A Memoir* by Willis Fletcher Johnson in 1907.

With little documentation and few details known, Sybil's life and her infamous ride has been greatly speculated on. My own book speculates, making it fiction instead of nonfiction, but is based on history and facts about the war, about Sybil, about horses, and even about fireflies. I borrowed historical details from other people, too. For example, Sybil and Rebecca used the clothesline to create a signal. A Patriot woman named Anna Strong, who implemented a similar technique by arranging clothing on her clothesline to reveal the location of hidden documents, inspired my characters.

Any inaccuracies or anachronism (I was surprised by how many words I wanted to use but could not use because they didn't yet exist in the 1700s!) are my own for the purpose of storytelling. The following is what I was able to conclude and mold into my story:

Sybil was born on April 5, 1761. At the time of her ride, she was one of eight children to Henry and Abigail Ludington. Her parents would later have a total of twelve children.

General George Washington tasked Sybil's father with building a spy ring and Sybil aided him, learning spy codes. Enoch Crosby was one of the spies who stayed in their home.

Henry Ludington's actions made him a wanted man and Sybil saved her father from capture by fooling Ichabod Prosser and a mob of Loyalists into believing her home was heavily guarded.

At the age of sixteen, Sybil rode forty miles through the night to muster Colonel Ludington's troops. While Sybil is often called the female Paul Revere, there are a few differences I'd like to make note of. Paul Revere rode a portion of his ride with two others. Sybil completed her ride alone. She was also half his age and traveled three times the distance. And, Sybil was never captured during her ride.

Sybil married at the age of twenty-three. While women during the Colonial era generally married then worked in their home, some sources believe that Sybil left the farm and opened an inn. She would've done so with her husband, as only men were able to obtain licenses for such professions during that time. While I left Sybil's future open-ended in the final chapter, I hinted at an innkeeper occupation throughout the novel as something that'd appeal to her.

In 1935, historical markers were erected along Ludington's route.

In 1961, Anna Hyatt Huntington sculpted a commemorative statue of Sybil. It's located at Lake Gleneida in Carmel, New York.

In 1875, a stamp was issued in Sybil's honor.

I'm happy to see the recognition Sybil has gained over the years, although her story is still largely unknown. Perhaps, though, you'll tell a friend about Sybil Ludington's story and we can help her become more known as a young heroine of the Revolutionary War.

And, if you want to learn about a second young star of the same war, may I recommend Dicey Langston, another horse-loving Patriot and spy.

**Jenni L. Walsh's** passion lies in transporting readers to another world, be it in historical or contemporary settings. She is a proud graduate of Villanova University, and lives in the Philadelphia suburbs with her husband, daughter, son, and various pets. Jenni writes nonfiction and historical fiction for middle-grade readers and adults, all focused on powerful women. To learn more about Jenni and her books, please visit jennilwalsh.com.

@jennilwalsh 🐦     @jennilwalsh 📷     @jennilwalsh 📘

@jennilwalshvideos ▶ YouTube